D0348540

"I alw
a big
my own," Jane told Kyle.

"So? Where are they?"

"Growing up, I changed my mind."

"Why?"

The icy sensation swam through her again. "My mom and dad had a strange marriage. Not very loving. I didn't notice until I was older. Marriage scared me, I suppose."

"Scared or scares?" His eyebrows arched, and he leaned forward, waiting for a response.

No sense in lying. "Scares, I guess."

His gaze riveted to hers. "How can you tell if the man you're marrying will be loving and gentle forever?"

"Exactly." She was astounded by his perception. "How does a person know?"

"Trust. Faith. Support. Prayer."

Books by Gail Gaymer Martin

Love Inspired

Upon a Midnight Clear #117
Secrets of the Heart #147
A Love for Safekeeping #161

GAIL GAYMER MARTIN

lives in front of her computer in Lathrup Village, Michigan, with her real-life hero, Bob. Growing up in nearby Madison Heights, Gail wrote poems and stories as a child. In her preteens she progressed to Nancy Drew–type mysteries. Apparently the love for suspense continued, since today she enjoys weaving mystery and suspense throughout her romances.

Gail is multipublished in nonfiction and fiction, with nine novels, five novellas and many more to come. Her Love Inspired novel, *Upon a Midnight Clear* (10/00), won a Holt Medallion in 2001. Besides writing, Gail enjoys singing, public speaking and presenting writers' workshops. She believes that God's gift of humor gets her through even the darkest moments and praises God for His blessings.

She loves to hear from her readers. Please visit her Web site at www.gailmartin.com or write to her at P.O. Box 760063, Lathrup Village MI, 48076.

A Love for Safekeeping
Gail Gaymer Martin

♥ *Love Inspired*®

Published by Steeple Hill Books™

If you purchased this book without a cover you should be aware
that this book is stolen property. It was reported as "unsold and
destroyed" to the publisher, and neither the author nor the
publisher has received any payment for this "stripped book."

STEEPLE HILL BOOKS

ISBN 0-373-87168-6

A LOVE FOR SAFEKEEPING

Copyright © 2002 by Gail Gaymer Martin

All rights reserved. Except for use in any review, the reproduction
or utilization of this work in whole or in part in any form by any
electronic, mechanical or other means, now known or hereafter
invented, including xerography, photocopying and recording, or in
any information storage or retrieval system, is forbidden without
the written permission of the editorial office, Steeple Hill Books,
300 East 42nd Street, New York, NY 10017 U.S.A.

All characters in this book have no existence outside the imagination of
the author and have no relation whatsoever to anyone bearing the same
name or names. They are not even distantly inspired by any individual
known or unknown to the author, and all incidents are pure invention.

This edition published by arrangement with Steeple Hill Books.

® and TM are trademarks of Steeple Hill Books, used under license.
Trademarks indicated with ® are registered in the United States Patent
and Trademark Office, the Canadian Trade Marks Office and in other
countries.

Visit us at www.steeplehill.com

Printed in U.S.A.

The Lord is my light and my salvation—
whom shall I fear?
The Lord is the stronghold of my life—
of whom shall I be afraid?

—*Psalms* 27:1

To: Kelly and Amanda
Thanks to: Birmingham Police Department
coordinator Frank Grant, Lathrup Village Police
clerk Patricia Christ and author Carol Steward
for answering my police questions,
and nurse Joe Fernandez,
who answered my medical questions

Chapter One

"**W**hy?"

Jane Conroy asked herself the same question a hundred times as she peered at her vandalized classroom and cringed at the crunch of glass beneath her feet. Two wide windows stood with shattered panes, their glass slivered on the wide marble sill and scattered across the floor. Textbooks lay in jumbled heaps around the room, and student desks had been strewn topsy-turvy.

Staring at the filthy graffiti covering the cream-colored walls, Jane clenched her fists. Anger and frustration vied for first place inside her. Her second day at Jackson Elementary, and she'd been violated.

Norm Skylar, her principal, compounded her wavering emotions. Since she'd reported the damage, he had treated her like a used tissue, something he'd like to discard and forget. And at the moment she felt about as useless.

New to the staff, she expected her principal's support rather than his condescending attitude—especially since her few weeks back in town hadn't given her enough time to offend a soul. Garnering her courage, she'd expressed those exact sentiments to him, but he didn't seem to listen...or care.

Skylar's reedy voice attacked her ear as he spoke in confidential tones with Kirk Brown from the central office, then glanced toward her with his placating glower.

To avoid his frown, Jane wandered to the teacher's desk and stared down at the floor, disheartened by the contents of her well-organized drawers now spread across the tile like trash. Crouching, she reached out to gather the glass-spattered supplies, but was jolted by Skylar's bark that shattered her solitude.

"Miss Conroy, leave that, please."

Like a reprimanded child, she snatched her hand from the heap of notepads. Heat rose to her cheeks, and she fell back on her heels and stood.

Skylar's frown nailed her to the spot. "The police will be here in a few minutes. When they're gone, you can pick up your things." Pinching his thin lower lip between his fingers, he pivoted back to his hushed conversation.

Police. Images swirled in her thoughts, and she cringed. Visions of the familiar policeman's uniform jackknifed her father's angry face into her memory. The defilement of her room wasn't enough. Now the debasing memories intruded on her morning.

Pushing the thoughts from her mind, Jane wandered toward the door to escape Skylar. With her thoughts miles away, she swung through the doorway and thudded into a broad blue-uniformed chest. With her nose against the badge, she froze, reliving her childhood panic. But when she raised her head, she focused on a pair of amused blue eyes set in a sturdy, handsome face.

"Excuse me," the officer said. His square jaw relaxed to a pleasant smile.

She collected herself. "My fault. I wasn't looking." But she certainly was now, marveling at his strapping size—tall and broad shouldered with an expansive chest.

Gaping at him, Jane realized neither of them had moved. Her cheeks tingled with rising heat, and she fumbled through her thoughts for a coherent sentence. "You're looking for the principal." She gestured toward Skylar, who stared in their direction.

Jane stepped aside to let the officer pass, but to her discomfort he shifted in the same direction. With a grimace, she shifted again, and he followed. They were like two people learning the Texas two-step. Addled, she stared at their toe-to-toe shoes, unable to look him in the eye.

In a flash, his hand rested on her shoulder. "You stay put, and I'll step around you, otherwise we may dance all morning."

Flustered by his touch, she held her place, riveted to the floor. When he passed her, she turned to watch him stride across the broken glass toward Skylar, who peered in their direction with thin, pursed lips.

When the officer reached Skylar's side, Kirk Brown said goodbye, shot past her and vanished through the doorway.

Jane stood back, watching as they discussed the break-in. Then, with a blast of expelled breath, Skylar headed toward the doorway. "I'll get someone on this shortly," he said to her with a nod to the disheveled room.

Jane followed him. "Is there anything I can do?"

Without comment, he turned and spoke to the officer. "You're through with me?"

"Right," the policeman said.

Skylar shifted his focus to Jane. "Find another room to work in until we get this cleaned up." He pivoted, gesturing into the air. "I don't know why these things happen to me."

Wondering what to do and where to go, Jane steadied herself amid the debris while the officer stood motionless across the room.

"I'm not sure where to begin," she said, gathering her bearings.

"Whatever you do, be careful of the glass." He sauntered toward her, then squatted and gathered a stack of file folders. He rose and placed them on her desk.

"Thanks. What can I do here?" she asked, gesturing to the clutter. The sunlight caught the prisms of shattered glass like sparkling fairy dust. "If I clean this mess, will I destroy the fingerprints?"

His silence turned into a chuckle. "I think you're safe. On a big heist like this one, we just check our list of local juvenile offenders."

"Juveniles?"

"That's the usual."

"This was done by students? But why?" She ran her fingers through her hair, envisioning cherub-faced third graders spray painting filth on her walls. How could they dislike her? Students hadn't attended yet. She'd only moved back to the Detroit area. Certainly, not enough time to upset anybody. "But it...but yesterday was my first day at Jackson."

"You mean this is the welcome you get? What about

streamers and party balloons?'' He gave her a playful wink. ''Knowing you isn't the issue. Kids just do things.''

With frustration, she plucked a textbook from the floor. The man was trying to be friendly, but the uniform bothered her. She had to admit he seemed mild-mannered, playful even. Still, her defenses rose, unbidden.

Avoiding the glass shards, she gathered the notepads and straightened. He hadn't moved. Tension tightened in her neck. ''Are you waiting for something?''

''Not really.'' His amused expression held its steady gaze.

Jane's stomach fluttered, and butterflies flitted through her limbs.

''So you're new in town.'' He extended his hand. ''I'm Kyle Manning…one of Redmond's finest.''

Tangled between interest and frustration, she grasped his strong fingers. ''Jane Conroy. One of Jackson's finest.''

''I don't doubt it for the world.'' He gave her a long, steady look before he released his grasp. ''Well,'' he said, shifting his feet and resting on one heel. ''I should hit the road and file this report.''

''And I should salvage my supplies,'' she said with a sweeping gesture.

He strode toward the door, but before he stepped into the hall, he hesitated. ''Now, do like the man said. Find another place to work before you cut yourself.'' He gave her a wink. ''Nice to meet you,'' he said and went through the doorway.

Jane stood for a moment staring after him, wishing he were anything but a police officer. She liked his gentle manner and his teasing way. The uniform and his behavior were a sad paradox.

Growing up with her angry, explosive, police officer father had left Jane with one resolute promise. Never would she be involved with a man who carried a weapon or wore a badge. The thought bristled up her back while the young officer's memory settled in her heart.

She refocused on the floor and stooped to right a desk drawer, then gathered the paraphernalia scattered about her feet and placed it inside.

"Now-ow...don't cut yerself there."

Jane straightened with breakneck speed and threw her hand against her chest.

A round-shouldered man in a gray work shirt and pants peered at her from the doorway. "I—I co-come to clean up the g-glass."

"Okay, thanks," Jane said, peering at his hangdog eyes and loose-jowled face.

He stepped into the room carrying a push broom in one hand and an oversized dust pan in the other. "Jus' call me Ch-Charlie," he said. Slack-jawed, he continued to watch her.

Jane hurried to gather her books and material. His fixed gaze sent an unpleasant sensation riding up her spine.

He leaned on the handle of the broom as if it were a crutch and watched her. "Jus' run a-along when you're—you're ready."

That's exactly what she wanted to do. She piled the books into her arms and scurried to the door. When she hit the hallway, she paused, then headed toward the teacher's lounge.

The room was empty except for an olive-skinned young woman with a full head of shiny, black hair.

Looking up from her poised pen, she smiled. "Hi. Have a seat." She gestured to the chair next to her. "I'm Celia Lopez. Welcome to Jackson Elementary."

"Jane Conroy. Thanks." The woman's sincere smile eased her with a calming effect.

"There's coffee on the counter." Celia pointed to a small alcove kitchen.

"Thanks. Maybe later." Jane piled her books on the round table and slid onto a chair.

"What a way to start your year, huh?"

Jane nodded. Except for Kyle coming to her aid, her confidence had been as sabotaged as her classroom.

"We're hall partners. Sorry, I didn't get a chance to talk with you yesterday," Celia said. "My room's next to yours."

Her classroom shivered through her mind, images of destruction and violence. "I feel so violated."

Celia frowned. "They didn't touch my room. I never understand why that happens."

Jane shrugged, wondering if this were God's punishment for her struggling faith.

Celia gave her a friendly pat on the shoulder, then lifted her coffee mug and sipped the pungent brew. "So what's happening with your room?"

"Charlie's sweeping up the glass."

"Good old Charlie," Celia said. "He's a mite slow, but the kids like him."

Jane agreed about the "mite slow." She shifted the stack of books in front of her to avoid speaking aloud.

Celia lowered her dark eyes and returned to her work. Silence fell over the room as Jane opened the lesson planning book with the intention of reviewing the material for tomorrow's first half day with her students.

But instead, Kyle Manning's image drifted into her mind. His friendly smile and teasing blue eyes shimmered in her thoughts like sunshine, but reality poked her again. The image of his uniform dropped a barricade against her warm thoughts.

Time ticked silently past. Finally Celia rose and piled her books into a stack. "Guess I'll get back to my room." She flashed an understanding grin. "At least I have one. Nice to meet you, Jane."

"Same here," Jane said, tugging her attention back to the textbook. But again her undisciplined thoughts reenacted her disconcerting earlier meeting with Kyle.

For years she'd watched her mother cower against her dad's angry words. Her Christian mother had raised her to trust in the Lord, but when Jane had called to God in her fear and confusion, she'd received no answer. Now her faith flagged and a challenging question surfaced: Why did God allow anger and violence to ruin the world?

With friendly greetings, teachers drifted in and out of the lounge, but the morning and afternoon dragged. Finally the wall clock hand's pointed to four. Jane stood and stretched, bracing her back with her palms.

When the door flew open, Jane looked up in surprise.

Celia paused in the threshold. "How would you like to join me for dinner somewhere?"

With no old friendships renewed, Jane longed for company. Without hesitating, she accepted the invitation.

"Great," Celia said. "I need to stop at the Teacher's Pet and pick up a few bulletin board supplies. Do you mind?"

''That's fine with me.''

''Whenever you're ready, then, let me know.'' She swung open the door and paused. ''Oh, have you checked your classroom? It looks almost finished.'' She grinned. ''Just holler when you're ready.''

Celia vanished, and Jane gathered her belongings, then headed down the hall to check her classroom. For the first time since she'd returned to Redmond, she felt adventuresome and optimistic. Her work would fill her time, and maybe Celia would become a friend.

Then Kyle nudged her thoughts. Never. A friendship with him was not possible.

Kyle couldn't believe his good fortune. As he stood at the restaurant entrance, Jane's bright curls caught his attention like a red flag. Glancing down at his jeans and a knit shirt, he wondered if she'd recognize him in his ''civvies.''

He'd spent the afternoon speculating how he might see Jane again, and seeing her across the room answered his question. Though they'd only talked briefly, she beckoned to his emotions. Maybe it was her uncertainty, or the faint flush that washed across her rounded cheekbones. She seemed shy. Or maybe lonely.

Perhaps his ''rescuer'' MO drew her to him. Whatever, he hadn't been interested in anyone particular in a long time. That morning, Jane Conroy had tugged at his heartstrings.

Hoping he wouldn't appear forward, he maneuvered around the crowded tables in her direction. The diner's unadorned decor seemed brightened by the petite redhead sitting in a back booth. When he reached her side, the young woman with her lifted a curious eyebrow.

He gave her a friendly nod and tapped his finger on Jane's shoulder.

She pivoted and looked at him with a puzzled frown. Then she drew in a deep breath, and the confusion in her sea-green eyes melted to surprise. "Oh, it's... you." A soft flush rose on her cheeks "I didn't recognize you without the uniform."

He winked, watching her flush deepen. "Undercover," he whispered. "I'm tailing you."

Wide-eyed, Jane studied him. "I like you better dressed this way."

He sensed something cryptic in her words. While he tried to sort out what she meant, Jane motioned toward her friend with the black hair and dark eyes.

"Celia, this is Kyle Manning," she said. "Kyle, Celia Lopez. She teaches second grade."

"Second grade. Well, now." Kyle grinned.

Celia leaned toward him. "Do you have recollections of second grade, Mr. Manning? If you'd care to join us, I'd be happy to listen."

Her flirtation was obvious. Kyle accepted the invitation, but instead of joining her he slid into the booth beside Jane.

When he was settled, Celia realized her wasted efforts. "So where did you two meet?"

"Kyle was the officer who came to my room this morning." Jane turned toward him. "Any news yet?"

"No, nothing before I went off duty. But don't worry. Someone out there will spill their guts." He realized his choice of words. "Sorry, that's a technical term we use at the station."

She laughed. He liked the easy sound, and he relaxed. Earlier, her subdued tone made him wonder if he'd offended her by stopping at her table.

"It's always a kid," he added. "They brag about their antics, and someone, usually a parent, does his or her civic duty and turns them in."

"Hopefully you'll know more the next time I see you," Jane said.

"Does that mean you'd like to see me again?"

This time, a deeper blush covered Jane's face. He studied her. She seemed attracted to him, yet uncertain.

Jane pressed her palms against her red cheeks.

Teasing, Kyle gave her shoulder a comforting pat. But he lingered a moment, enjoying the feel of her slender arm beneath the cloth of her silky blouse.

"It's the red hair," she said.

Celia chuckled. "Great excuse."

Kyle eyed the situation. "I hope you didn't mind that I plopped down here. Did I interrupt anything?"

"Not at all," Celia said. "We're just two hungry people who don't want to go home and cook."

Kyle eyed Jane for approval. "Then it's okay if we're three hungry people escaping the same fate?"

"Sure," Jane said with a hesitant smile.

Intrigued, Kyle longed to know more about this confusing woman.

They quieted, comparing menu items, and finally Kyle signaled the waitress who took their order.

As they dined, casual conversation rattled on. But as they ordered coffee, Celia opened her wallet and dropped some bills on the table. "I don't want to put an end to this evening, but I have some things to do." She grinned at Jane. "I'm sure Kyle will keep you company." She gave him a meaningful arched eyebrow, rose and left them.

Kyle leaned back, enjoying the silence and the privacy Celia had offered them. But with her departure Jane grew quiet.

After coffee was served, Jane looked up from her cup with a sigh. "I enjoyed the company tonight. I've felt pretty much alone since I came back to Redmond."

"Back to Redmond?" Kyle asked. "You mean you lived here before?"

"Grew up here." She lowered her eyes. "My mom died a couple of months ago. In July. Dad died years ago."

"Sorry to hear that." Kyle's thoughts flew immediately to his own parents.

She looked up. "I'm their only kid. An orphan at twenty-nine. With a house sitting here empty and a mediocre teaching job up north, I decided to move back home. Things sort of fell into place." Her misty eyes softened.

Her nostalgia reminded Kyle of his own loss. He gripped his coffee cup, fighting his desire to reach over and comfort her. "It must be hard losing parents. I'm pretty close with mine. It took me a while to move out of my folks' house." He chuckled. "But I have my own place now."

"A house?"

"Apartment." He rested his elbows on the table and folded his hands in front of him. "My life's not very interesting."

Jane arched her eyebrow. "How can you say that? You're a police officer."

"I mean, my family came here after I got out of high school, and I followed along. Never moved away. Nothing adventurous." He flinched. Admitting he was in a rut wasn't the way to impress a woman.

"Mine isn't, either," Jane said. "Any brothers or sisters?"

When he heard her question, the old sadness shot through him. He paused to recover from the unexpected emotion. "I had an older brother. But Paulie died in the military. It was a difficult time for us. Especially my folks."

"I'm sorry. I shouldn't have asked."

"No, please, it's okay." He touched her arm, loving the softness of her flesh against his fingers.

Jane lowered her eyes and traced the design in the plastic tabletop with her fingernail. "I remember how we felt when my dad died." She appeared lost in thought, then lifted her head. "Was he young? Your brother?"

"Twenty-one. I was just a kid. Eight, maybe. He was much older than me. And my idol."

A heavy lull settled over the conversation. Kyle struggled to think of something to say that might lighten the mood, but the emotion weighted the air.

"Do you live alone?" he asked finally.

Her face brightened. "Just me and Wilcox."

"Will Cox is….?" His full stomach plummeted. She lives with someone.

A coy grin curved her generous mouth. "Cat," she said.

"Cat?" Reality seeped into his mind, and a laugh rose from his chest. "Oh, Wilcox is your cat."

She nodded. The smile remained.

The food bill arrived, and Kyle grabbed it before she could. "Don't say a word. I enjoyed having your company for dinner."

She acquiesced, and after he settled the bill, they stepped outside. Kyle drew in a long breath of the late-summer air, mingled with her sweet, tangy fragrance like lemonade and sugary ripe melons. He filled his lungs and lifted his gaze to the heavens.

A wash of purple and orange splashed across the horizon, and the hint of a quarter moon rose in the darkening sky. Too early for stars, he lowered his gaze to Jane's glimmering eyes.

He grasped her elbow and guided her toward the parking lot, enjoying her nearness. He'd become a police officer to defend and protect people. Jane aroused that need. She was alone and vulnerable. He longed to watch over her...and he wanted to be her friend.

They walked close together, wrapped in silence. Heading down a parking aisle, Jane pointed to her car.

But Kyle's seasoned eye spotted trouble. He faltered.

"What?" Jane asked.

Wanting to make sure, Kyle hurried toward her vehicle. At close range he confirmed the truth.

"Looks like you've got a problem."

Chapter Two

Jane's stomach tightened, and she followed the direction of Kyle's finger to the left side of her sedan.

"I'm beginning to take this personally," Jane moaned. Her car sat at a strange tilt with two flat tires.

Kyle crouched, checking around the tire rim. When he rose, he held two bent nails. "Could be an accident," he said.

A relieved sigh shot from her, and she watched as he knelt again and studied the next tire.

When he rose, a frown rutted his face. "Forget what I said. Looks like someone may have done this intentionally."

He circled the adjacent cars, investigating the automobiles and checking their tires.

"The others look okay. I'd guess the perpetrator was interrupted."

"You mean this is another coincidence?"

"It happens. Kids decide to fool around and let air out of tires. They pick cars at random. Sometimes, they're interrupted."

Far-fetched, she thought. One coincidence maybe, but two? An unsettled feeling fluttered through her. She shrugged. "Whatever. But it makes me nervous. So now what do I do?"

His face softened, and he rested his hand on her shoulder. "Hey, remember? I'm one of Redmond's finest."

"Okay, I'm waiting."

His wink didn't ease her much, but he was right. If she had to be in trouble, being in the company of a policeman was the best place to be.

"Wait right here," he said, gesturing for her to stay put. "Help is on the way." He turned and headed through the parking lot.

She watched him go, wondering what she would have done if she had been alone. And she really was alone. She had no one really. Basked in the warm evening air, a cold, lonely shiver traversed her frame.

When Kyle returned, he carried a metal canister, waving it as he walked toward her. "Air in a can. Pretty handy, huh?"

"You're on duty even when off, aren't you? A regular lifesaver."

"Just can't help myself." He grinned and knelt beside the tire.

The first tire rose from the ground, then he proceeded to the second. When Kyle stood, he chucked her under the chin. "Now this'll only get you to a gas station. It's a partial fill."

"Thank you, kind sir, but I realize that." She ruffled from his insinuation. She had a brain.

"Just a little reminder. Don't take it personal."

His gentle comment and good nature filled her with

shame. "Thanks," she said, wishing she didn't like him.

"I'll follow you to a gas station and fill those tires for you. That's 'beyond the call of duty,' you realize."

"I'll owe you."

"And you can be sure I'll collect."

His words sent a tiny flutter through her chest until it knotted with reality. The last thing she wanted was to fall for a cop. As she climbed into her car, she struggled with wavering emotions.

Kyle leaned into the open door. "There's a station right up the road. Follow me."

Jane pulled out of the parking lot behind him. Ahead, she could see his silhouette through his rear window. He sat tall in the seat, and she envisioned his powerful arms grasping the steering wheel. Yet Kyle's kindness and compassion gave his strength a new twist. A gentle giant...and so different from her father.

A half mile up the road, Kyle pulled into a gas station. Jane followed, aiming the nose of her car for the air pump sign displayed on the side of the garage.

Before she could climb out, Kyle had already grabbed the hose and squatted beside her wheel.

She joined him, and when he shifted to the second tire, she followed, watching him add the air and check the tire pressure.

Looking down at him, she grinned. For a change, her five-foot-two-inch frame was standing above his strapping six-foot-plus body.

He moved to the third tire. "Now you know you'll need to keep an eye on those two over there and make sure you don't have a puncture."

"Yes, sir," she said, but mentally skidded to a halt, harnessing the grumpy remark that rose in her thoughts.

She dragged her fingers through her hair, wishing she could enjoy his warm geniality without feeling guilty.

Too much had happened. The move, the new job, the loneliness. The town rekindled her nagging memories, and she seemed to have lost her spirit. Yet she was strong. Maybe not "muscle" strong, but strong in defending convictions. That hadn't changed. She'd never back down on anything if she knew she was right.

Kyle shifted to the final tire as Jane's attention was drawn to a man, wearing a station uniform and ambling her way. Caught by a feeling of familiarity, she peered at him. His eyes widened as he focused on her, and hesitant recognition struck them at the same time. Excitement rifled through her.

"Perry?"

The man's jaw dropped, and he squinted as he neared her. "Jane?"

With a simultaneous nod, they rushed toward each other, arms open wide.

She nestled her face in his oil-scented shirt, then stepped back and examined his face. He'd aged, but he looked like the same old Perry Jones she knew from high school.

Perry beamed. "Jane, you look wonderful. As young as you did in high school."

A rush of pleasure shot through her. "Sure. Keep it up, Perry. You don't look much different yourself."

He tilted his head forward, pointing to a small balding spot on his crown. "No? What about this?"

"Minor problem." She squeezed his arm. "So what've you been doing with yourself…besides working here?" She tapped the station emblem and his name on the shirt.

He looked at the stitching with a grin. "Dead give-away. Well, I started college and decided it was fool-ish. I always loved working on cars—so I applied for state certification, took the test and I'm doing what I love."

He held her out in front of him, then shifted his gaze to Kyle who was standing at the air pump. "You married?"

"No." She glimpsed at Kyle, wishing he weren't a police officer and wondering what he'd think if he'd heard Perry's assumption. "I had two flats, and Kyle offered to help."

She appreciated Perry's familiar, yet changed face. "Seems strange being in town. I just got back a few weeks ago, and I'm already teaching at Jackson Elementary."

"I thought you were living up north."

"I was, but my mom died. The house was empty and…well, it's a long story."

Perry's pleased expression faded. "Sorry about your mom." He glanced down at the cement. "Your dad, too. I remember that."

She looked into his saddened eyes, amazed that someone from her past shared her sorrow. "So are you married? You and Betsy were pretty thick before I left."

"We've been married for ten years. Can you believe it? We have two boys, Kenny, seven, and Tommy, five."

"That's great." Betsy married. The thought seemed alien. They had been good friends throughout high school, but time and distance intervened.

Finally Kyle sauntered over and joined them. "Perry, do you know Kyle Manning?"

Perry extended his hand. "I don't think so."

Kyle shook his hand, and the conversation continued until Jane realized she was delaying both men. "I have to get going, but tell Betsy I said hi and for sure we have to get together and talk over old times. I thought I might be the only one left here in Redmond."

"Betsy'd love to see you, Jane. We're in the phone book. Give us a call."

She agreed, and Perry returned to his work.

Jane turned to Kyle. "I didn't mean to hold you up. Thanks for your help." With her eyes straight ahead, she avoided his direct gaze and stared at his chest. "I appreciate this...more than I can say." Her fingers, of their own volition, pushed back her curls.

"What are cops for?" A flicker of amusement tugged at his lips. "Or friends for that matter. And you can be sure I'll collect."

When she arrived early the next morning, Jane's classroom didn't look bad, but the room reeked of paint. At nine o'clock, twenty-eight eager faces greeted her. By the time she reviewed the class rules and procedures, explained needed supplies and learned a little about each of them, the half day had ended. With the last student out the door, she left the building for lunch.

When she returned in the afternoon, Kyle was waiting for her in her desk chair. A teasing smile played on his lips as she eyed him from the doorway.

"What's this?" he asked. "The first day back to school, and you're already playing hooky? *And* you didn't lock your classroom door."

She tried not to gape at him while her mind devised reasons why he had dropped by. She'd spent the past evening thinking of him, despite her reservations, and wondering if she'd really see him again. Now here he was in front of her.

"I was at lunch," she said.

"Okay, I'll give you lunch, but what about your door?"

"I forgot."

"The first lesson in safety. Lock the door." He rose from her chair, ambling to the edge of the desk and leaning there. "Your tires were still full this morning?"

She nodded. "Right, so that means it wasn't a nail puncture."

"Doesn't sound like it. Kids can use a nail to open the air valve. Just vandalism, like the mess here."

Curious, she eyed him. "Did you hear something?"

"Just the facts, ma'am." He lifted his hand as if to touch her chin, then lowered it. "A couple of junior high boys. We nabbed them today."

"Really?" A sense of relief edged over her. Maybe everything had been a coincidence.

"Apparently, one of the culprits bragged to a kid who told his parents. The father called one of the guilty boys' parents. They found the near-empty spray cans hidden somewhere and checked with the police. Sure enough. Case solved."

"I'm glad. To be honest, I was getting paranoid."

"Can't really blame you. But things happen."

"Thanks for letting me know," she said.

He rested his hand on her shoulder. "You don't think I came here just to tell you about the vandals, do you?"

The warmth of his hand flowed down her arm. She peered at him with curiosity.

"I came to collect."

Collect. A flutter like hummingbird wings settled in her chest. "So what will this cost me?" Jane asked.

"How about dinner sometime?" He dropped his hand from her shoulder.

"You want me to *take* you to dinner or *cook* you dinner?" She'd pay him off...and then, hopefully, she could get him out of her mind.

"Both sound great."

Both! There was paying a debt, and then there was taking advantage. She struggled for a response.

"But buying *you* dinner is what I had in mind."

"Buy me dinner?" Confused, she faltered, shifting through his words. "But that's not—"

"Not fair? Okay. Next time you take me."

His deep blue eyes captured hers, and her emotion plummeted into the whirling depths of his gaze. "Next time? I haven't agreed to this time. Plus you've already paid for my dinner."

"Then you owe me two dinners."

Her stomach rose and fell like a child's yo-yo. What would Principal Skylar say if he saw Kyle hanging around? She glanced into the hallway. "Okay, I'll go. Now I have to get back to work." She opened her desk drawer, pulled out a memo pad and jotted down her phone number.

He glanced at the paper. "Thanks, I'll call you."

Ambling through the doorway, he gave her a wink that sent her stomach tumbling.

Days later, with shopping bags nestled in their arms, Jane and Celia stopped at a mall food court. After they ordered, Jane's thoughts drifted to her class, in particular, to one sad girl named Lena. After observing her for a few days, Jane was concerned. Something was wrong.

When the waitress delivered their meals, Jane bit into her deli sandwich, her mind whirring with questions. The mouthful settled in her stomach like a lump. "You had my students last year, didn't you?"

Celia nodded.

"Did you have Lena Malik?"

"Sure. Having problems?" She glanced up from her salad.

"She's a nice kid, but downgrades herself terribly. She refers to herself as 'dumb.' Any idea why?"

"Wait until you meet her father." She peered into Jane's eyes "And you will."

Her father? Jane's chest tightened, and a hunk of bread lodged in her throat.

"The kid's afraid of Papa, I think," Celia said. "Big bushy mustache, penetrating dark eyes. Not big in stature, but in presence. You'll meet him." ·

"I can't wait."

When they finished eating, they walked outside to a lighted parking lot. The autumn days had shortened and darkness settled into long shadows on the concrete.

Celia stood outside the mall door. "Where did we park?"

Jane looked over the dusky sea of automobiles. "I know where I parked. Back at the school. Where you parked is a good question."

They scanned the lot and agreed in a general direction. After wandering, they found Celia's car, stowed their packages and headed back toward the school.

"How about dropping me at the library?" Jane asked, checking her wristwatch. "It should still be open. I want to pick up a couple of books, and it's only a block to the school. I can walk to my car.''

"Are you sure? I can wait.''

"No, that's silly. I'll be a few minutes. I need the exercise anyway.''

Celia didn't argue, and in a few moments they pulled in front of the library. Celia tugged on the trunk latch as Jane climbed from the car and pulled out her three shopping bags, then rapped on the window.

Celia lowered it a few inches.

"Thanks for the nice evening,'' Jane said.

"You sure you're okay?''

Jane nodded, plastering a confident expression on her face.

Dreary thoughts had edged into Jane's mind during dinner. She sensed someone watching her, but when she glanced around she saw nothing unusual. Then she chided herself for being silly. Her vandalized classroom and the flat tires had set her on edge. But she bolstered her courage. "Thanks, I'll be fine.''

Celia waved and pulled away.

As Jane turned toward the library, an overwhelming feeling of uneasiness ran through her. She breathed deeply and glanced around her. Shadows lengthened along the walk, but the street looked quiet and safe. She ran her free hand through her hair, thrust out her chin, pulled back her shoulders, then hurried into the library.

Jane left her packages with the librarian who stored them without complaint. Jane moved along through the book stacks, following the Dewey decimal numbers.

Crafts. She needed ideas for her social studies unit. Or maybe some interesting true stories about historical figures the students would be studying. Whatever, she wanted to spice up her lessons. Keep the third graders interested, yet learning.

She moved toward the back of the towering stacks. Kyle jutted into her thoughts, and she longed to have him at her side.

Hurrying along, she found the 700s, pulled a book from the shelf and flipped through the pages. A shiver of fear ran through her. She spun around, scanning the adjacent aisles. Was someone watching her?

She peered through gaps in the bookshelves, detecting someone peering at her from the next aisle.

The book dropped from her fingers.

She sprinted to the end of the stacks and with the fear of a frightened bird, her eyes shifted and her heart hammered against her chest. The aisle stood empty.

A ragged breath tore through her. Imagination. She had let the situation get the better of her. She was foolish. Returning to the shelf, she snatched up the book she'd dropped and carried it with her.

With her eyes panning like a searchlight, Jane selected a few books and, controlling her tremors, carried them to the checkout counter. As the librarian processed the books, Jane modulated her voice. "Did you see a man pass a couple of minutes ago?"

"A man?" She glanced at Jane. "Not that I recall." She stuck her books through the computerized system, slapping the covers closed, and slid them across the counter to Jane.

When she stepped away, the librarian called her back. "Your packages." She reached under the counter, pulled the three bags from below and handed them to her.

Jane thanked her and headed toward the exit. Yet, as she approached the door, she paused. Darkness shrouded everything beyond the library lights. Tonight she needed her faith, a faith that had kept her strong through so many difficult times during her childhood. But she'd discarded her trust in God, determined to deal with life by herself. She took a deep breath and pushed open the door.

Descending the three stairs to the sidewalk, Jane turned toward the elementary school and her car. With swiftness she stepped along, passing beyond the comforting lights.

Darkness blanketed her. Her heels clicked along the cement sidewalk, and her chest tightened with each stride as she gained momentum.

Movement sounded behind her, a muffled footfall in the grass. A sound like the snapping of a branch struck her ear. She faltered and glimpsed over her shoulder. Nothing. Was it her imagination?

Picking up speed, her legs stretched until she was running. Yet, amid the rustling of her shopping bags, a distinct sound echoed behind her. Fearful, she swung around to see a dark shadow dart into an alleyway.

Her heart jackhammered, and panic knotted every nerve. Flying along the sidewalk, her chest ached. The rustled footsteps continued a short distance behind.

The school loomed in front of her, and her car waited at the side of the building. She dashed around the corner. The sedan's silhouette rose ahead of her. Her own gasps filled her ears.

Her door remote?

She plunged her hand into her pocket, grateful to feel her keys nestled safely inside. With a fleeting glance over her shoulder, she raised her keyless remote, hit the button and heard the comfortable beep.

With her uncontrolled momentum, she thudded

against the car door. In the faint light, she groped along the cold metal and grasped the door handle as a shadow fell across her arm.

A hand clamped down on her shoulder.

A scream tore from her throat.

Chapter Three

"**M**iss Conroy, what's wrong with you?"

Jane flung out an elbow and flattened her back against the car, her breath coming in gasps. She gaped into her principal's shadowed face. "Mr. Skylar, y-you scared me. What—what are you doing here?" She squinted into the darkness.

"What are *you* doing? I'm going to my car." He held a briefcase in front of her face in the dim light. "I forgot my work."

She cringed. "I'm sorry. Someone was—was following me."

Skylar scanned the darkness. "Following you? I don't see anyone. I think your imagination has gotten the better of you, Miss Conroy."

"No, not my imagination." She raised her fist to her pounding heart. "I stopped at the library, and I'm positive…I was followed. I think someone was watching me in the library."

"If you went to the library, why are you parked here?" He peered at her in the faint light.

She explained, but his attitude suggested she had done something wrong. "It's only a short walk from the library to the school."

"It's been a long day, Miss Conroy. I'll wait here until you get into your car. How's that?"

She nodded, but his patronizing tone frustrated her. She opened the door, and when the dome light brightened the interior, she glanced into the back seat. Empty. She slid inside and locked the door.

Skylar followed her on foot while she rolled slowly through the parking lot. Before she pulled onto the highway, she halted. In the brighter streetlight, she saw him shake his head as if she were a blithering idiot.

Could Norm Skylar have been chasing her? Logic said no. He wasn't out of breath as she had been, but how had he sneaked up on her? Why hadn't he called out when he saw her running? A multitude of questions rattled inside her head.

Peering into the darkness, Jane searched for an automobile that might be following her. Nothing seemed out of the ordinary. But how could she know for sure? Pulling into her driveway, she braked and froze. Staring at her front door, she was gripped by fear.

Jane grasped the house key and mentally measured the distance. How long would it take to get inside? Her packages and books could stay there until morning. But how long for her to turn the key and get inside?

Shadows muted the ground, and only a shrouded moon shed a dim light against the house. The shrubs and trees could hide anyone. She glanced over her shoulder and squinted into her yard, her heart pounding like a judge's gavel to bring order to her wavering world.

"Oh Lord, help me." Despite her lack of active

prayer in the past years, the words tumbled from her lips without thought in times of trouble. And though she thought God found her hopeless, she knew the Lord listened.

Headlights inched down the road. Jane's heart rose to her throat, her breath stifled in her chest. As the car neared, she recognized the bubble on top, and a stream of halted air shot from her lungs. Could it be? She waited, her blood coursing.

The squad car swung into her driveway, and when the headlights faded, Kyle's face brightened the darkness through the windshield. Why had he come? She knew. He was her prayer—answered. He stepped from the car, and Jane flung open her door and barreled into his arms.

He held her against his chest. "Jane, what's wrong? Why were you sitting in the car?"

"I was too petrified to get out. I'm so grateful you showed up." Her gasps pounded against her ears.

"What happened?"

He held her closer, and a sense of safety calmed her. As a child, her mother's comforting arms had protected her. The memories washed over her like a sad lullaby.

Catching her breath, Jane began her story. Kyle listened in silence while he gathered her books and packages, then followed her into the house.

She crumbled into a nearby chair, her anxiety rising again. "I don't understand this, Kyle."

"Are you sure someone followed you?"

"I might have a vivid imagination, but not that vivid. Someone followed me."

A frown wrinkled his smooth forehead, and he held her in his gaze as he sat.

"I'm positive," she said again, dragging her fingers

through her hair and hoping to see his face filled with understanding. Instead, he looked dubious.

"Did you think it might have been a library patron? Just a coincidence?"

"Why do you think it's a coincidence? You explained the classroom away, but how about my tires? Sure, in the library stacks, I could be wrong, but not on the street. I knew he was following me. I was scared to death."

"Did you catch any details? Was it a male?"

"I think. He was tall...like you." A sigh shuddered through her. "I was running. I know he was following me."

Kyle patted her hand. "Jane, I think you have a bad case of nerves. The tires made you edgy, and now you're imagining all kinds of things."

"Do you think I'm a lunatic? I know when someone follows me. I'm not crazy, Kyle."

"I didn't mean it like that. Someone may have been behind you for a perfectly logical reason. You saw what you saw, but the man wasn't necessarily following you."

She closed her eyes to ease the pounding in her head. How could she explain? She was so sure. Yet...Kyle was experienced, and he...

A sigh of resignation escaped her. "Maybe you're right. I even suspected Norm Skylar when he scared me in the school parking lot. I don't understand. I've never been a wimp."

He gave her arm a squeeze and rose. "You're not a wimp. Everyone gets frightened on occasion. Even me."

She couldn't imagine him frightened. But she was.

"Could you wait a minute while I get my head together?"

"Sure. Take all the time you need."

Her eyes filled with gratitude, and Kyle watched her as she headed down the hall. He plopped his back against the love seat cushion and gazed around the room—feminine, but practical. Cozy, he'd call it.

His thoughts drifted to Jane's situation. Could he be wrong? Her room was vandalized by kids. The tires? He didn't know for sure. And now the stalker. Could the man have been some innocent guy heading home or…could she be correct? Was it—

"Whoa!" The word shot from his mouth, and he jerked backward as an object plopped into his lap. His heart raced, far over the speed limit. He struggled to gain composure while the culprit purred up at him.

Embarrassed at his reaction, he caught his breath and grinned at the furry creature in his lap. "You must be Wilcox. You scared me, man. I think I've caught a case of nerves from your mistress."

Wilcox gazed at him with chartreuse eyes and purred loudly while Kyle rubbed the cat's fur.

He tousled the cat's head, addressing the fur ball. "You know, Wilcox," he said, staring into the cat's eyes, "hopefully it won't be long before we'll be on a first-name basis."

As he completed his sentence, Jane entered the room, eyeing him with curiosity. "So you've met my buddy."

Kyle set the cat on the floor. "Yep. He and I have already become quite attached. He told me to call him Will."

"Oh, really."

Her tone made him smile. She had changed into

jeans and a long T-shirt. A pair of furry slippers hugged her feet. He leaned back, ready to explain why he had dropped by.

As if reading his mind, she arched an eyebrow. "So, now that I've calmed down a little, why are you here? And—" she lowered her voice "—how did you know where I live?"

"A police officer can find out anything. Since I was passing by... I, ah, well, I remembered we need to make dinner plans."

He'd promised to *call.* She nodded, watching him squirm.

"Is Saturday good for you? I'm off duty this weekend."

Jane marveled at his unexpected discomfort. He seemed as nervous as she was. "Saturday's good."

His shoulders relaxed. "Great, but I'm still holding you to that home-cooked dinner."

Tension knotted in her chest. He was moving too fast, though part of her longed for his friendship. "We could come back for coffee after dinner."

"And pie." He gave her a bright smile. "Peach or berry—any kind of berry. Oh, and ice cream. Warm pie, cold ice cream."

"That's a pretty straightforward order," she said.

"My dad taught me to be honest. He's a minister."

As if hit in the stomach, she flinched. "A minister's son?" The words flew from her mouth, and her mind wrestled to recover from the surprise. She grabbed her first available thought. "Then I'll expect good things from you."

"Don't expect much. My dad's the minister." He gave her a toying wink. "I'm just your average sinner. Stole a softball from the five-and-dime when I was a kid. Threw spitballs over the balcony at the movies. Cheated on a question on one of my exams.''

Jane listened to his confession. She pictured hers like bloodred neon across her forehead. *Trying to protect my mother, I prayed my father would die.* That was one of her secret, guilt-ridden sins. One God had granted. She could never tell anyone, especially a preacher's son.

He rose and brushed her cheek with his fingers, his eyes warm and natural as summer rain.

She wanted to fall on her knees, confessing what a horrible person she really was. But before she made a fool of herself, Kyle straightened himself and took a backward step. ''Suppose I'd better get back to work.''

Relief mingled with fear. She lowered her eyes.

''Will you be all right?''

Afraid to look at him, she focused on her hands, clasped in a tight knot. ''I'll be fine. Thanks.''

She watched his feet shift to what she assumed was a defensive stance. An idiosyncrasy she'd notice. ''I'll check around outside before I leave—just to make sure.''

''Thanks.'' She rose and followed him. ''See you on Saturday, then?''

''About six.''

He touched her arm and the gentle warmth radiated to her heart.

''And lock your doors when I leave,'' he said.

She agreed, and when he left, she waited by the window while he wandered around the exterior of the house, then pulled away. Was he worried about her, or was his ''police officer'' persona being naturally cautious? She didn't know which she wanted.

* * *

Anticipating her evening with Kyle, Jane stopped on the way home from work Friday to buy the ice cream. On Saturday afternoon when she started the pies, she'd thought about the situation.

Her mind had swung like a pendulum. She wanted his friendship. She didn't. Never had she been so paradoxically wishy-washy. How could one man motivate and confuse her so easily?

Since she learned Kyle's father was a minister, she kept asking herself the same question: What am I doing? And the same answer repeated often in her thoughts. It's a hopeless situation. I'll never, ever get seriously involved with a police officer. Especially one whose father is a minister.

As Jane rolled the last crust, Kyle's boyhood list of sinful discretions filled her mind. They sounded naive and chaste compared to hers. The day she fell on her knees and prayed her father would walk out of their life, even die, filled her with shame. The fourth commandment resounded in her mind. "Thou shalt honor thy father and thy mother."

Somehow in trying to defend and honor her mother, she'd dishonored her father. Each time the scene rose in her thoughts, the paradox wrought her with guilt, leaving her weighted with sorrow and exasperation.

The commandments were impossible. Didn't God realize sometimes a person had to break one part of a commandment to keep another? Could a minister's son understand that? And could Kyle ever comprehend her feelings about policemen?

Jane forced her mind to push aside her quandary. By evening, she was eager to see him. When she caught the flash of headlights across the living room wall, she hurried to the door and pulled it open before he rang the bell. "Well, if it isn't Redmond's finest."

She heard Kyle chuckle. "Great. That saves me a lot of time trying to impress you."

Jane stepped back, motioning him into the house.

"Have a seat. I'm just about ready."

She hurried out of the living room and stood in the bathroom, talking to herself in the mirror. Besides his striking appearance out of uniform, she had the first-date jitters. Her cheeks glowed, announcing her excitement. She took deep breaths, and when she felt in control, she joined Kyle, and they left for dinner.

As the evening progressed, Jane found conversation easy, yet selected. Both seemed to be holding back pieces of themselves. When they returned to her house, Kyle shuttled her to the front door like a bodyguard.

Inside, Jane gestured to a recliner. "I'll put on some coffee."

Instead, Kyle followed her to the kitchen. "I'd rather stick with you...if that's okay?"

Concern ruffled Jane's thoughts. His wariness set her on edge. He'd tried to pooh-pooh her fears. Did he sense something wrong or not? Fearing his response, she was afraid to ask.

Kyle leaned against the counter and watched her pull cups and plates from the cabinet. When he caught sight of the pies, his face beamed like a child. "You made those for me?"

His strapping size and his boyish charm were a paradoxical delight. The tension she'd felt moments earlier slipped away.

He peered at the two pies. "Strawberry, and what's this one?" He poked his finger at the crust until it broke through. Ogling his jam-coated fingertip, he licked away the syrupy fruit.

She eyed his tongue playfully capturing the filling, and felt a tingle roll through her chest.

"It's peach, in case you can't tell." She grinned, seeing his pleased expression.

"You're a pal." He put an arm around her shoulder, giving her a fleeting hug. His nearness wrapped her in a safe cocoon and the heady scent of his aftershave enveloped her senses.

After cutting the pies, Kyle helped her carry the cups and hefty slices covered with ice cream into the living room. He sat on the love seat, placing his mug on the small coffee table, and Jane followed, sinking into a nearby chair. In silence they dug in to the homemade confection.

Wilcox worked his way around Kyle's ankles with a soft purr, then placed his paws on Kyle's legs and stared at him with bright green eyes.

"Why me?" Kyle asked, faking a whimper.

"You two are on a first-name basis. Buddies always share."

She peered at the cat. "Hungry, Wilcox?" Jane rose, and the cat wound around her feet as she coaxed him to the kitchen.

When she returned, Kyle looked uneasy. She sensed he wanted to talk and wondered if the topic was what had preoccupied him, on and off, throughout the evening.

Resting his elbows on his knees, Kyle leaned forward and stared across the room. "When I was filing the vandalism report down at the station, someone said your dad had been a police officer." He lifted his eyes as if questioning her.

A prickle of tension edged along her shoulders. She'd been right. Something had been on his mind. "Yes, he was."

His expression reflected disappointment, a response she didn't understand.

He glanced toward the family photographs displayed on a bookshelf, then rose and ambled across the room. He studied the pictures and picked up a photograph of Jane's parents.

When he returned it to the shelf, he lifted a picture of her father in uniform. "I've seen your dad's picture at the station. The captain has a wall of photos in his office." He replaced the frame and faced her. "Your father was killed in the line of duty."

Jane nodded and set down her plate. She clamped her teeth together, hoping he'd not dwell on the subject.

"I was surprised this afternoon when it dawned on me he was your dad." He stared at Jane, then turned again to the photograph. "Red Conroy. Red. That's what they called him."

Jane smoothed her own red hair with trembling fingers. "Yep, red hair like mine."

"Conroy. I never connected the name. I've heard stories about Red Conroy."

Fearful, Jane cringed. Had Kyle heard the rumors that her father had been mixed up in something crooked? Shame washed over her. What would he think of her?

"I'm surprised you never told me." Kyle sent her a puzzled look and wandered back to his seat. "Quite a hero."

She shuddered. She didn't want to hear the word *hero*. She wrestled her frustration. "You know the saying, 'A prophet in his own country isn't appreciated.'

He was just Dad to me.'' She lied, and the anguish slithered down her back.

''I'd liked to have known him.'' His gaze traversed her face. ''I'm sorry, Jane. I guess I've upset you.''

She stared down at her clenched hands pressed into her lap. He'd upset her more than she could say. She'd lived in shame that someone would learn that her father had done something wrong. Shame that weighted on her conscience. And a sin for which she couldn't atone. So often she dreamed of having the awful memories vanish, the fear and sorrow gone. Dreams didn't work. She needed the Lord.

''Jane?''

Pulled from her reverie, she refocused.

He stared at her with puzzled eyes.

''I'm sorry, Kyle. No, it's just me. I still have a hard time thinking about my dad. It's my problem.''

He shook his head. ''I should have been more sensitive.''

''My dad's death was followed by a lot of unpleasant speculation. Nothing proven. No evidence. Just rumors, but the memories are painful.'' Hearing the admission surprised her.

''Do you want to talk?'' His head tilted, his gentle gaze captured hers.

She shook her head. But she wasn't telling the truth. She did if talking would release her of the black memories.

''Leave it to me to put my foot in my mouth.''

She wanted to apologize or to explain, anything to rid the air of the discomfort. But before she decided what to say, he filled his fork with a hunk of pie.

''Better this, than my foot.'' He chuckled and shoveled the generous bite between his teeth, then licked his lips. "Now that's better."

His gentle gaze was filled with understanding.

"Let's talk about you...and this pie. Then later we can talk about you...and the pie in the kitchen."

Celia caught up with Jane on the way into the building Monday morning. "Couldn't wait to tell you about the great guy I met."

Her face glowed, and Jane couldn't help but smile. "So where did you meet this great guy?"

Celia reached across Jane and flung open the school door. "I went to this little restaurant near my house for dinner." Following behind, Celia released the door and caught up to her. "So I sat alone, and this nice-looking guy—his name's Leonard Hirsch—came in right after me and sat at a table next to mine. Well, you know how it goes—"

"No, I don't, but I'm sure you'll tell me," Jane said, fighting off a laugh at her friend's exuberance.

And Celia did, every detail.

"And you have a date for..." Jane inserted the key and swung open her classroom door.

"Tonight."

"Congratulations."

"Thanks."

"Miss Conroy."

A small voice caught Jane's ear. She turned and looked into a young boy's upturned face.

"Yes?" she asked.

The child raised a paper bag to her. "I'm s'pose to give you this."

Jane glanced at Celia, then back to the boy. "You are?"

"Uh-huh."

"From Mr. Skylar?" She arched a questioning eyebrow.

"No, a man in the parking lot." The child shoved the bag toward her. "The man leaned out the car window and said, 'Give this to Miss Conroy.'"

With caution, she took the package. "Thanks." Her hands trembled as she held the paper bag away from her body. Something wasn't right.

"Okay." The boy gave her a final look and headed down the corridor.

Celia gaped at her. "What's wrong?"

"I don't know, Celia. I'm afraid to look in the bag." Unbidden, her arm moved forward, distancing herself from the plain brown sack.

Celia looked confused. "What's in it? You're as white as a ghost."

Students pushed past Jane into the classroom with noisy greetings, and she smiled down at them, but her mind was miles away. "Remember when I thought someone followed me the other night?"

Celia's eyes widened. "Yes, so what's up?"

"Nothing, I guess." She nodded toward Celia's room. "You have kids waiting."

"Great. Leave me hanging." She glanced toward her room. "I suppose I'd better let them in."

She swung around to leave.

An overwhelming fear clutched Jane as she peered at the sack. "Celia, wait."

Celia halted and turned back. "What?"

"Could I ask a favor? Would you glance inside and make sure it's nothing terrible. I don't have the heart." Her mind whirled with the possibility of something evil and foul clutched in her hand. But why?

With a tolerant shrug, Celia took the bag, opened the top and glanced inside, but Skylar's voice halted her comment.

"Ladies, you have students waiting," he snapped. "Celia, why are your students outside the room?"

"I was checking something for Jane."

He arched an eyebrow. "And?"

"And I'm going to class now." She jammed the paper bag into Jane's hands. "It's okay, Jane." She spun around and sped toward her classroom.

Skylar stared at her, and she turned and entered the classroom.

As the students pulled out their work, Jane set the package on her desk and stared at it. Foolish. What could be so dangerous in a small grocery bag? She took a deep breath, controlling her tremors, pulled open the top of the sack and looked inside.

An old, dog-eared book lay in the bottom. Surprised, she shrugged and pulled out the volume.

When she turned the book over, the title struck her between the eyes. *Fun with Dick and Jane*. A torn piece of paper stuck out from the pages, and she flipped it open.

Circled in black marker, two sentences rose from the page. Her legs trembled as she peered at the words.

See Jane. See Jane run.

Chapter Four

Disbelief knifed through Jane. She looked from the primer to her students, then instinctively to the hallway. Her heart gyrated as she focused on Charlie standing outside her doorway, leaning on a push broom. When she caught sight of him, he ducked his head and scooted out of sight, pushing the broom as he went.

Her pulse was pounding so loudly in her ears she didn't hear Sara speaking to her. When the child tapped her arm, Jane jumped.

"Sorry, Sara, did you want something?"

"Are you sick, Miss Conroy?" Her young face twisted with concern.

"Oh, no, Sara, I'm fine."

"You look funny."

Jane forced a lighthearted laugh. "No, I was thinking about something. I'm just fine." She drew in a wavering breath and sank into her desk chair. Her hands still clung to the book. She closed it and slid it into her center desk drawer.

The students gaped at her with curiosity. Jane struggled to think of something she might tell them, maybe something funny, so they'd laugh and not sense her concern. Not only would a laugh help the students, she needed something to pull the shards of fear from her own mind. As soon as she could arrange a break, she'd call Kyle.

At lunch break, Jane left Kyle a message that she needed to see him—or at least talk to him. He was on police business, the desk officer said, and she didn't dare tell him it was an "emergency" although her racing pulse told her it was.

During lunch, Celia hovered over her until she told her the story, but Jane waited until the end of the day to take the book and the rest of the information to Skylar. She didn't know what she expected him to do, but maybe now he'd believe she wasn't hallucinating.

She waited outside his office while he spoke to another teacher, and when he finished, she leaned into his office. "Could I talk with you a minute?"

"What is it?" he asked. "I have a meeting at the central office in fifteen minutes. Can you make it quick?"

Jane wondered if she could convey her fear and frustration in a couple of minutes. She walked into his office with the primer clutched in her hand.

"I know you think I'm deluded, Mr. Skylar, but I'd like to show you something." She handed him the book, explaining how it came to her.

"Do you remember last week when I ran to the parking lot? Well, look," she said, pointing to words circled in the book. "Here it says, 'See Jane run.'"

He pursed his lips. "And? What am I supposed to get from this, Jane?"

"Don't you see the connection?" Her body tensed with frustration. "'See Jane run.'" She pointed to the words. "It's right there. Someone sent me this book...on purpose...to scare me."

He shook his head as if he was speaking to a confused child. "Don't you think you might be jumping to conclusions?"

Her body tensed with irritation. "In what way am I jumping to conclusions?" She struggled to keep her voice calm. Why couldn't he see a connection? She wanted to scream in his face, but she'd learned as far back as Sunday school a soft voice turns away anger.

"Let's try this out." With a smug expression, he leaned back in his executive desk chair. "A parent is cleaning an attic and finds this old elementary school primer. 'Now what can I do with this?' asks the parent. 'Ah, Johnny has Miss Conroy this year. Maybe she'd enjoy having this book.'"

He peered at her, apparently expecting some conceding response. But instead she had questions of her own. "And if that's the case, why didn't 'Johnny' bring me the book instead of some man handing it to a *fourth* grade boy in the parking lot?"

"Perhaps he forgot to give it to Johnny as he left for school, but he passes this way going to work, and instead of leaving his car and searching for you, he hands it to a student in the parking lot." He glowered at her. "I don't know, Miss Conroy, but I have a meeting to attend, and I have to leave." He rose and pinned her with his look. "A third-grade teacher with some off-the-wall ideas resigned last year. I hope with my encouragement I don't have another on my hands."

He tugged his briefcase from his desk and swished past her out the door. She sat in the chair for a moment staring at the empty space, wondering what had just happened.

Later that evening, Jane sat alone, disappointed that Kyle hadn't at least called and wondering if she might be as foolish as everyone seemed to think. In her mind, she retraced the strange occurrence. The vandalism wasn't directed at her personally, and as far as she knew, the tires weren't, either…though they may have been.

The person who followed her? A fluke, maybe? An innocent man hurrying behind? Like Skylar said, the "Dick and Jane" book might have been a parent's gift. A coincidence. But when the incidents were added together, they became more suspect. Why couldn't Skylar see that?

Wilcox jumped into Jane's lap, and her heart beat double time. Her nerves were frayed, and she wondered if she'd ever feel relaxed again. Lately, the only time she felt safe was with Kyle.

Pulling her hand over the cat's fur and hearing his calming purr soothed her. She dropped her head against the sofa. When she was a child, she always talked to God when she was afraid or had troubles. But so much time had passed since she'd turned to the Lord that she felt ashamed asking for help now. Still, she needed God's help. Jane closed her eyes.

Lord, I've drifted from You. Tell me how I can live within Your commandments. Protect me from the evil I'm sensing around me and the fear I'm feeling. Before an "Amen" left her lips, the cat's body stiffened. He leaped to the floor, his back arching and ears flicking. Jane held her breath.

Then came the knock on the front door. Stay calm. Ask who it is.

She rose and eased her way to the door, standing as far back as she could and still be heard. "Who's there?"

"Take a guess."

Kyle's cheerful voice sailed through the door, and Jane pulled the latch open, happy and relieved he had finally come.

"Kyle." She pushed the storm door aside. When he entered, she marveled at his good looks. Tonight he was out of uniform, dressed in casual slacks and a soft green pullover. "Am I glad you came! Did you get my message?"

"Sure did. Sorry I took so long to get here. I was tied up in court and didn't get your message until a while ago." He paused, studying her. "I didn't know it was an emergency." He clutched her shoulders and faced her. "Something's wrong, Jane. What happened?"

His concern tumbled through her as warm and caring as a mother's lullaby. "I got a little gift at school today."

He frowned. "What kind of gift?"

"A book." She motioned him into the living room.

"A book? That sounds innocent enough."

She swung around to face him. "*Fun with Dick and Jane.* Makes you think, doesn't it?"

"You mean the old elementary school book?" His face twisted in confusion, and he slid into a chair. "I don't get it. Well, I get the *Jane* part."

She sat in the love seat across from him. "Whoever sent it, put a marker in the book and circled the words, *See Jane. See Jane run.*"

His eyebrows raised. Then he lowered his head and stared at his shoe. Finally, he looked up with understanding eyes. "I see it. The other night when you thought you were followed, you were running."

"Yes," she whispered, pleased he understood, but hating to hear him make the connection. She bit the corner of her lip. "I went to Skylar today, but he pooh-poohed me. Said the book was probably a gift from a parent who found the primer in his attic and thought I'd enjoy it." She studied his face, wondering if he agreed. "I don't think so. Do you?"

He squinted. "That seems far-fetched. Let me see the book. Might be some identification inside."

Her heart sank. "I didn't think, Kyle. I left it at school. The thing upset me so badly I threw it in my desk drawer to get it out of my sight." She swung her arms apart with frustration. "I didn't think to look through it."

"I'll drop by tomorrow and take it to the station. I'll have them look it over."

Humiliation edged through her. "I should have thought, I suppose."

Kyle swung from the chair to the cushion beside her. He slid his arm around her shoulder and covered her hand with his free one. "Look, you've been under a lot of pressure. Whether things fit together or not, I know you're trying to sort them out. But...you can't play detective. Leave that to us."

The comforting pressure of his palm enveloped her with a sense of security. What would she do without him?

"Try not to worry." His tender look calmed her.

He moved his hand and massaged the tension in her neck. Then, shifting to a better position, he gently kneaded her rigid shoulders while his thumbs circled the neck muscles until her entire body yielded to his tender ministrations. A healthy silence hung on the air before he spoke.

"How's that?"

She released a grateful sigh. "Wonderful."

"I'm glad." He lowered his arms and drew her around to face him. "Now, I stopped by for a second reason."

He'd jolted her attention, and she waited.

"Before I ask, I want you to know that you can refuse. You won't hurt my feelings...much."

Her pulse did a two-step. "Now that you've set me up, what's the question? Looking for that free dinner?"

His light chuckle rippled the air. "No, but it has to do with dinner."

She shot him a quizzical grin. "You're cooking me dinner?"

"Better yet, my mom is."

Jane looked at his eager face, feeling her cheeks sag and sending her grin on a journey.

His pleasure faded, obviously noticing her reaction. "My folks invited me for Sunday dinner, and I asked if I could bring you along."

"Me?" She tried to smooth the scowl wrinkling her forehead, but it won out.

"Sure...and don't look so tense. I have to keep my eye on you, don't I? How about it? Mom's the best cook in town."

"She is, huh?" She playfully arched an eyebrow, hoping to make up for her scowl.

He squirmed. "Naturally I haven't tasted your talents in the kitchen yet...except for those great pies."

"That's a quick bit of finessing." This time a real grin made it to her face.

"Call me Mr. Tact."

Vying for time to think, Jane used their nonsense chatter to evaluate his invitation. On one hand, she felt flattered that he'd invited her to meet his parents. On the other, with Kyle being a minister's son, she felt like a kid being paraded to the new friend's house for parental approval.

"What happens if they don't like me?" she asked. "Maybe they'll think a stalked woman is a bad influence on you."

"How bad an influence? I like a challenge."

She shook her head, her mind slipping from the humor to reality—dinner with a police officer and at a minister's house. The dilemma was mind-boggling. She fidgeted.

Her hesitation finally hit home. He eyed her. "Are you letting me down easy?"

"Not exactly, but you hardly know me...well enough to take me home."

"But to know you is to love you. And don't forget I'm best friends with your pal Wilcox."

She grinned at that. "Now, that is true."

Jane really like Kyle—more than liked. Despite her reservations, he was very different from her dad, but.... She watched Kyle's expression. He looked so disappointed, she didn't have the heart to refuse.

"Okay," she said. "I guess I can handle it, but you'll have to give me a quick lesson on eating dinner at a preacher's house. You know...the proper protocol."

"I'll bring along a copy of my 'preacher's proper

protocol pamphlet.'"' He gave her wink and rose. "Try saying that six times."

She grinned as he leaned over and placed both hands on her shoulders.

"I'll pick you up on Sunday around four," he said. She nodded.

Kyle slid his hand to her hairline and ran his fingers along the nape of her neck.

She flinched, but this time he smiled, realizing his fingers tickled.

"Hmm? Now I know how to torment you," he said.

If he only knew, she thought, caught in his tantalizing gaze. "Remember, we have to be *good* influences on each other."

His eyes glinting with mischief, he skimmed his fingers to her jaw, then moved them upward and caressed her cheek. Surprising her, Kyle leaned forward and brushed his lips where his fingers had been.

The warmth spread over her cheek and down her neck. She opened her eyes and saw his strong jaw twitched with emotion.

He stayed bent above her and, over and over, he murmured a quiet litany. "Be good. Be good." Then he straightened his back and gave her a tender smile.

Like a robot, she followed him to the door, and he left without a word being spoken.

She stood rooted to the spot, staring at the closed door. Finally she raised her hand to her cheek and crumpled into the nearest chair. What am I getting myself into?

Jane slept poorly that night, thinking about the *Dick and Jane* primer...and Kyle's gentle kiss. Pulling herself out of bed the next morning, she knew the school day would prove difficult.

When she reached her classroom, the locked door was ajar. Jane peeked through the opening and froze. Charlie stood behind her desk with his hand inside a drawer.

"Charlie," she said, pushing open the door and stepping into the room. "What are you doing?"

"O-oh, l-last night when I cl-cleaned, I saw y-you needed...ch-chalk." He pulled the small container from the drawer. "I—I brought you a-a box."

She faltered as shame smothered her. "Thanks, Charlie." She thought of no fitting words to apologize.

His jowly face sagged. "I—I'm sorry if I d-did s-something wrong." He edged away from the desk.

"No need. I'm sorry for snapping."

Without another word, he edged toward the door and with one backward glance, he left.

Her heart sank. The stress was undoing her.

Needing reassurance, her thoughts shifted to Kyle. His presence gave her a sense of well-being and made her feel safe. She longed for him to pull her against his broad chest and help her feel normal.

With a slam and bang, students charged into the room and roused Jane to action. Always eager for the weekend, her class acted up on Fridays. That day was never easy and definitely not conducive for learning. But when the bell rang, Jane reined in their exuberance, knowing in a few more hours the weekend would be hers, as well.

Her lunch break finally arrived and she grabbed her sack and headed toward the lounge. Partway down the hallway, she heard her name and paused, her pulse kicking into high gear. Turning, she smiled at Kyle.

"I forgot you were dropping by," she said.

"Forgot? You mean that's all the impression I make on you?"

As she reached him, Kyle gave her a boyish pout. The look melted her. She cast aside her unsettling thoughts, wanting to reach up and kiss his full, inviting lips. "It's been a bad day," she said.

"Bad?"

She motioned for him to follow her back to the room and on the way, she told him the incident with Charlie. "The poor guy was trying to be nice."

"Don't blame yourself, Jane. You've been on edge and suspicious."

Jane stopped in her classroom doorway and faced him. "You mean paranoid? Delu—"

He lifted his finger and pressed it against her lips. "No. Wary. Careful. *Normal* reactions." He let his hand drop to her shoulder and spun her around to face the room.

She headed for the desk and Kyle followed.

"Here," she said, pulling the primer from the drawer, "the infamous book."

She dropped it into his outstretched hand. "Dust it for fingerprints while you're at it."

"My, my, do we sound skeptical?"

His look made her heart sink. She was acting terrible. First Charlie. Then Kyle. "I'm sorry."

"No apology necessary." He stood a moment without speaking. "How about some fresh air?"

She glanced at her watch.

"Only a minute or two," he said. "It'll do you good. Bring your lunch."

Wisdom told her to say no. What would the staff—worse yet, what would the students think if they saw her being led outside to a patrol car? But today she didn't care. She nodded and followed him outside into the sunshine, warmed more by his thoughtfulness than the lovely autumn weather.

Except for the bright spot with Kyle, the rest of the day plodded along. Jane looked at the wall clock and breathed a sigh. Only fifteen minutes before the final bell. The weekend would be hers. Even dinner on Sunday with Kyle's folks was beginning to sound good.

As she pulled her focus back to the children, a movement at the door caught her attention. Mary Campbell, the principal's secretary, stood in the hall holding a slip of paper.

For a moment, anxiety nailed her to the chair. Then, pushing her concern aside, Jane stepped to the door. Without a word, Mary handed her the note and retreated down the hallway.

Jane peered at the memo. Celia had warned her about her student's father. Lena Malik's dad would be waiting for her in the office at three-fifteen. Her stomach churned. On a Friday afternoon? What did he want? She tried to guess. With her classmate's additional help, Lena was progressing well. That's all she could report.

When the bell rang and the last student exited, Jane straightened the top of her desk and gathered her belongings. As she stepped toward the door, Celia swung into her room.

"Ready?" Celia asked.

Jane rolled her eyes. "I have an appointment with Mr. Malik."

"On Friday?"

Jane nodded.

Celia followed her into the hallway while she locked her door. As they walked toward the office, a question popped into Jane's thoughts. "Who's the teacher who taught third grade last year?"

"Dale Keys. Why?"

"Skylar mentioned him. He said he hoped he didn't have another off-the-wall teacher on his hands. What does he mean?"

Celia shrugged. "Dale? I don't know. He was quiet and didn't hang around with anyone. Only Larry Fox. He's the art teacher." She scowled, thinking. "Dale didn't seem happy at Jackson. Maybe he was expecting too much from teaching."

"Maybe. I was just curious." Jane glanced at her watch. "I'd better hurry. I'm due there in a minute."

With her heart thumping and her nerves on edge, Jane hurried inside the office. Mary nodded toward the small conference room, and Jane drew a deep breath before entering. When she did, Sam Malik was sitting as rigid as a statue.

"It's always nice to meet parents early in the year," Jane said, pushing a pleasant expression to her face. "I'm pleased that you've stopped by." Liar. Mentally she reminded God how difficult she found keeping all the commandments at the same time. "Now, what can I do for you?" She faltered when she saw Malik's glowering face.

"My daughter tells me you're making a spectacle of her in front of the class." His dark eyes pierced hers.

"I what? Would you mind explaining?"

"Oh, come now, Miss Conroy. Let's not play games."

"Mr. Malik, I'm not playing games. I've done everything I can to make Lena feel comfortable. She's a lovely child, just very quiet and shy. But I'm pleased that she's made real strides already this year in math. As you know, it's very difficult for her.''

"Yes, you've certainly pointed that out to the whole class.''

"I have?'' Anger sizzled up her back.

"I'm tired of your innocent look, Miss Conroy. Sitting my daughter in the back of the room with another student is not my way of helping a child who belongs in special education. She should be taught by a teacher, not a fellow student.''

With her frustration growing, Jane responded like a witness facing a jury, carefully selecting her words and trying to remain calm. "Many children sit at the back tables for rewards, as well as special help, Mr. Malik. I haven't singled your daughter out in any way. The other girl is her friend, and they work together.''

Afraid of losing courage, she snatched a breath and plowed ahead. "And I've checked her records. She's not a special ed student. She's shy, but once she gains confidence, I believe she'll be able to learn with the group rather than needing individual help.''

"And what makes you an authority on *my* daughter? She's always been backward. You're prejudiced, Miss Conroy. You're making a spectacle of her and getting some sort of pleasure from it.''

Jane's blood curdled. She wanted so badly to tell him that *he* was the one causing his daughter's problems, belittling her and calling her "dumb.''

"I'm sorry you feel that way,'' Jane said. "I'll be happy to arrange for her to be tested again by one of our special education staff.''

Malik slapped his fist on his stocky knee. "I think

the whole bunch of you are in cahoots. You toss the problem back and forth, protecting each other.''

Frozen with fear, Jane stared into Malik's fiery eyes, his face twisted in contempt.

''Then feel free to have her tested on your own,'' Jane said. ''You can call the intermediate school district, and I'm sure they can advise you. Or use the Yellow Pages. Whatever makes you confident that Lena's getting a fair assessment. In my judgment, her self-esteem needs bolstering. Once she has some confidence, she'll learn like any other child.''

With the speed of light, Malik rose, knocking the chair against the wall. ''I can see that you're no more cooperative than that other woman. I'd hoped Lena would have a male this year, someone with brains in his head.'' He pointed his finger in her face. ''You'll hear from me again. You can be sure of that.''

In a flash, Malik bolted from the room, leaving Jane shaken and confused. Her tense shoulders relaxed as she released a breath from her throbbing lungs. She had no idea how to deal with someone that unreasonable.

Chapter Five

Trying to decide what to wear put Jane in a quandary. Never in her life had she felt so tense about a dinner date. But then, she'd never been asked to the home of a man's parents before—at least, not since her teenage years. That was a long time ago.

Though she was anxious to tell Kyle about Sam Malik, she feared it might turn the evening into a "downer." It could wait.

After one more search through the closet, Jane settled on an earth-tone print skirt, which draped nicely over her hips, and a rust sweater that complemented her red hair. She wanted to look especially right for Kyle's folks. Not too prim, but proper. With makeup in place, she dressed, then paced.

When Kyle arrived, he grinned and handed her a trifold paper.

She laughed at his concocted protocol pamphlet and read the inside message, "Be yourself and smile." She waved the fake brochure under his nose. "You think this will work?"

"No doubt about it. Wait and see."

A short time later when she walked into the Manning residence, Jane knew Kyle's advice had been perfect. His parents welcomed her with as much charm and friendliness as the parsonage decor.

"How nice to meet you," Ruth Manning said, giving Jane's hand a firm squeeze. "It's so rare for Kyle to bring home a friend." She chuckled. "In fact, since he got a place of his own, he never does."

Kyle's father opened his arms in a wide generous welcome. "I'm Paul Manning. So nice to have you visit us. Please, sit." He gestured to the sofa and turned his attention to his wife. "Mama, give this young lady some soda or juice."

"I'm fine, thanks," Jane said, taking the spot he'd indicated.

Kyle plopped down beside her. "Have a seat, too, Dad. We're fine."

He did as Kyle suggested while Ruth excused herself to return to the kitchen.

Jane's admiration was drawn to the large, yet gentle, man, and she wondered why she had been hesitant to accept Kyle's invitation. Looking at his father, she could imagine what Kyle would look like twenty years from now. Handsome as Kyle, yet his seasoned face was etched with years of compassion and concern for others.

Dressed as he was in a plaid flannel shirt and navy trousers, to Jane, he didn't look like a pastor.

"Kyle tells us you've had a couple of bad scares since you've moved back," Paul said.

"Well…one at least." Jane related the things that had happened. "Kyle said the classroom and tires were probably just kid's foolishness.'' She rethought her comment. ''At least, the vandalized room was.''

''Well, it's not a very warm welcome to Redmond. We've always had a peaceful community here, but lately I don't know.'' He scratched the back of his head, thoughtfully. ''I've been preaching on that exact subject. I suggest we all keep our eyes wide open for the enemy. He appears in many forms. Even as a co-worker or friend.''

His comment slid uneasily down Jane's spine, but she nodded pleasantly, preferring the conversation to focus on the community rather than on her.

She felt Kyle squeeze her arm. His ability to sense her discomfort was astounding.

''And where do you worship, Jane?''

As if her thoughts of discomfort spurred his question, Jane froze. No doubt, Kyle felt her tense.

With quick thinking, she mustered a vague answer. ''My family always went to First United over on Downing.''

''Really? That's wonderful. I know Pastor Johnson well.''

Feeling cornered, she swallowed and tugged out her honesty. ''I'm afraid I don't know him. I haven't attended there in quite a while.''

''No? Then Kyle will have to bring you over to First Community some Sunday. We'd love to have you.'' He leaned toward her and grinned. ''You can hear one of my infamous sermons firsthand.''

Jane felt another white lie coming on. ''That would be nice.''

Her words lay heavy in her heart. She studied God's word and believed in Jesus. But after years of struggling with the feelings about her father, she'd become frustrated. She'd broken so many commandments—in bits and pieces. How could she explain that to anyone?

To Jane's relief, before Kyle gave her another comforting squeeze or his father asked another question, Ruth bustled into the living room and halted the conversation. She headed for the low coffee table and set down a tray containing glasses of fruit juice along with a plate of cheese and crackers.

"Help yourselves now," she said. "I'm putting the final touches on dinner. Everything should be ready soon."

Jane liked the woman. Her dove-toned shirtwaist, accented by a perky bow, hung over her slightly plump hips, and darker gray hair curled softly around her pleasant face. Jane thought she made the perfect pastor's wife: friendly, gracious and soft-spoken.

Ruth pivoted and returned to the kitchen while Paul offered Jane a small plate. She felt obliged to place a couple of crackers and cheese wedges on the dish, though she preferred to save her appetite for the dinner she could smell drifting in from the kitchen: roasted pork, seasoned with rosemary, she guessed, and maybe apples.

The tantalizing aroma aroused her hunger. Pleased that the snacks had suspended the conversation, she joined the others and nibbled a cracker.

While Kyle filled his plate, he studied Jane's reaction to his parents. Before arriving, she'd seemed nervous, but her demeanor had changed when she met them. He was pleased that she'd relaxed.

He loved watching her…being with her. Something about Jane captured his interest. Captured him. His thoughts had been filled with her since they'd met.

At first he thought it might be that he was a cop,

concerned for her safety and intrigued by her vulner-ability. But today he had no question. It was the spir-ited redhead herself. It was Jane.

He was pleased he'd finagled a Sunday dinner in-vitation for her. On the telephone, his mother's voice had raised ten decibels when he asked if he could bring a woman friend along. No doubt his imaginative mother was already planning their wedding. He'd rec-ognized the eager sound in her voice. Kyle often won-dered if his parents thought once he married that he'd find a safer career. He hated to disappoint them.

Drawn again to Jane, Kyle tried to cover his stare, but he wondered if she realized he was watching her. Each time she glanced at him, his heart skidded over a speed bump.

Surreptitiously he gazed into her misty green eyes, admired her satin skin brightened by her dress color, and marveled at her ginger-red hair. She reminded him of an Indian summer afternoon: warm, natural and in-viting.

When his dad had asked Jane about her church af-filiations, Kyle had felt her body tense. He wondered why she was uncomfortable with the question. As Kyle's thoughts drifted, his father's words dragged him back.

"…Terribly sad day when we learned our older son, Paul Jr., died in the Middle East. So you can under-stand how difficult it's been for us to have Kyle join the police force. Different perhaps, but dangerous just the same."

Jane didn't respond, but Kyle saw her nod.

"But then a dad's wishes don't always weigh a lot."

Kyle's heart sank. He knew he had to honor his father, but he also had to quiet him. "Dad, this isn't the time to talk about this. We have company."

"Sorry, son."

Sadness weighed on Kyle's shoulders as he watched discomfort fill his father's face.

Paul's head lowered, and after a thoughtful pause, he turned to Jane. "Forgive me for grumbling. Sometimes my heart gets weighted with worries, and I forget we have guests. Like I said, Redmond's been a safe community, but more and more the problems are finding their way into the suburbs, and I get fearful for our town."

Kyle flinched when he heard his father's words. They were only half-true. His dad really feared for him.

"Prayer, Dad," Kyle said. "Put your burdens on the Lord. How many times have you told me to do just that?"

Kyle's comment did the trick.

Paul flung his head back with a laugh. "I guess you're right, son. I should heed my own advice."

Jane understood exactly what Kyle's father meant. Her father's life always seemed pressured by many things. She sensed her mother's unhappiness so often, perhaps because of her father's temper, but her mother seemed to love him and feared for him, no matter what. Jane never understood their relationship.

"My father was a police officer, too." Unbidden, the words exited her mouth and her pulse skipped through her veins. "I know my mother felt exactly like you do each day my dad went to work."

Paul's attention sharpened. "Where did your father work?"

"Right here in Redmond. He died a few years ago—"

"No, don't tell me." He straightened in his chair, grasping the arms, and leaned toward Jane. "Red Conroy. Was he your father?"

Dread filled Jane. "Yes. Did you know him?"

He didn't answer for a minute, as if his mind soared back in time. "I knew your father fairly well." His head pivoted slowly from side to side. "Red Conroy. I can't believe it."

Kyle edged forward in his seat. "How did you know Jane's father, Dad?"

Paul stared into space, then, as if jolted from his reverie, he looked at Kyle. "Oh, we served on a couple of…committees together. Involved in some community projects." Paul stared at Jane. "Red Conroy's daughter. Well, I'll be."

An eerie premonition washed over Jane. A feeling that there might be more to the story. She curbed her speculation. Her imagination had gotten out of hand, and she wondered if she could tell fact from fiction. And deep inside, she wasn't sure she really wanted to know.

On the way home that evening, Jane fell silent. She wanted to tell Kyle about her meeting with Sam Malik, but she hated to ruin the wonderful day she'd spent with him without worrying about threats and stalkers. Before she decided what to do, Kyle broke the silence.

"You seem quiet. I hope my dad didn't make you uncomfortable with all his talk."

"Uncomfortable? No, I like your folks. They're real people. Natural and unpretentious. They treated me great. Like I belonged there."

Kyle slid his hand up her arm. "You did belong there. I invited you."

"You know what I mean." She gave him a teasing poke. "And both hands on the steering wheel, please."

When they pulled into her driveway, thoughts of Lena's father were still troubling her. She hadn't uttered a word.

"Would you like to come in a minute?" she asked.

He turned off the motor and opened his door. "I'd hoped you'd ask."

He hopped from the car, and before she knew it, he'd circled the car and opened the passenger side. "Madam," he said, motioning for her to exit, as if he were a nobleman or knight. He was her knight, in so many ways.

She stepped from the car and Kyle slipped into stride with her up the porch steps. Inside, Jane poured them each a soda, and they settled in the living room.

"Okay. What's up?" Kyle said.

Jane's head jerked upward, and she gaped at him. "What are you talking about?"

"You've had something on your mind all the way home."

His uncanny ability to read her mind gave her the shivers. Realizing it was useless to hide anything, she told him about Malik. "He said I was embarrassing his daughter and I was prejudiced." She told him her response and Malik's reaction.

Kyle listened, his forehead creased and his fingers tapped against his leg as if he were ready for action. "I don't like the guy," Kyle said when she'd finished.

Jane frowned. "Me, neither, but he's a parent. What can I do. I know one thing for sure. He doesn't think much of women."

"How do you mean that?"

"He said he'd hoped that this year Lena would have

a man with some brains. Or something like that. I suppose he assumed she'd have Dale Keys."

"Who's he?" Kyle asked.

"The teacher I replaced. I learned his name from Celia. Skylar made reference to him the other day. He said he hoped I wasn't as off-the-wall as he was."

"Skylar sounds like a great guy. I don't like him, either."

Jane laughed. "You don't like anybody, do you?"

"Sure I do," he said, his tender gaze gliding across her face.

Jane's chest tightened as he lifted his fingers and caressed her jaw. She remembered the fleeting kiss he'd given her, and tonight, a new longing jolted her. She wanted to be kissed. But this time really kissed.

As if he heard her, Kyle leaned forward and without restraint, Jane lifted her mouth to meet his. The brief touch was soft and warm, but left her breathless.

"Believe me?" Kyle asked.

She knew she should understand, but she didn't.

"I like you…more than words can say."

A flutter rose in her chest and rippled down her arms. "I like you, too" was all she had the breath to say.

Monday morning, Jane pulled the trunk latch near her feet, then climbed out of her car. Lifting the trunk lid, she hauled out the craft materials she'd purchased for her class, wondering how she'd get them all inside.

She managed to gather the load into her overburdened arms and trudged into the school. Inside her room, Jane piled the packages on the desk, and as she stored away the supplies, thoughts of Lena occupied her mind.

Jane was torn how she should treat the little girl:

ignore her individual tutoring or continue as she had been. Thinking of the child's needs after the class began, she threw caution down the drain and invited the two girls to work in the back of the room as usual.

When lunchtime came, Jane hurried to the lounge, but hopes of a break were shattered. Before she could finish her lunch, Skylar's secretary appeared and handed her a note to see him immediately. Swallowing the distress that overtook her, she headed to the office.

When Jane left Skylar, she'd been stunned by their meeting. She'd been scrutinized from all angles without one saving grace. He'd berated her. He'd grilled her. Had she shown prejudice? Didn't she know how much retesting would cost the school district? Next time, he said, he'd sit in on her meetings. She'd sat like a punished child, shocked and unable to respond with any intelligence.

But his last comment topped them all. She could hear his voice. "If you see Dale Keys around your classroom, tell him I'd like to speak with him. I hear he's in the building."

"Sure," she'd said, hesitating. Was Skylar thinking of giving Keys back his job? She slammed her thoughts shut. She was getting paranoid.

Following lunch, the students settled into their seats, and the afternoon began with her half-eaten sandwich churning inside her. While the children worked on spelling, Jane tried with little success to concentrate on paperwork at her desk.

Pausing, Jane looked toward the door and saw a man watching her from the hallway. He saw her look and he signaled. Jane rose and tiptoed to the doorway.

"May I help you?" she asked, stepping outside.

"I'm Dale Keys," he said, extending his hand. "This was my classroom."

"Jane Conroy," she said, clasping his fingers. "I've heard."

"Really? Just thought I'd introduce myself."

"Nice to meet you." Jane inched toward her room. The man seemed normal enough to her. Why did Skylar call him off-the-wall? Then she remembered. "Oh, and I'm supposed to tell you that Mr. Skylar said you should stop by his office."

"Really?" A long, deep exhale rattled from his throat. "I'm surprised. He and I didn't get along."

"He can be rather opinionated." She figured her comment was tactful.

Dale tucked his hand in his trouser pocket, and Jane listened to the metal jingle while she waited for his next comment.

He didn't say a word, and hearing the children's whispers, she glanced into the classroom and tapped against the doorjamb. The room quieted. "I'd better get back inside," Jane said.

"I suppose I should see what Skylar wants."

After they said goodbye, she reentered the classroom, thinking of Skylar's negative attitude. The guy seemed okay.

After the final bell, she stood by the door while the children filed out, when Celia gestured for her to wait.

Jane nodded, then went inside to straighten her desk and gathered her belongings.

"Ready?" Celia asked, standing at her doorway.

"Just about." She headed for the closet for her handbag, wondering why Celia had a silly smirk on her face. "So why the grin?"

"Aren't you curious?" She giggled. "I had another date with Len. I didn't get to tell you at lunch."

"Great. One of these days I'll have to meet him."

"I'm sure you will. When I'm more comfortable with him, maybe we can plan a double date or something."

"Sounds good." Jane pulled her handbag from the closet and carried it back to her desk.

Celia followed her. "I take it you survived your conference with Skylar."

"Barely."

"That bad."

As she relayed the details of her meeting, Jane searched inside her handbag for her car keys. They weren't there. Concerned, she felt in her pockets.

"Lose something?"

"My keys. I always keep them in my purse."

She emptied the contents on her desk and rifled through them. "They aren't here." Anxiety rattled her as she ran her hands over her clothing again. "Not in my pockets, either."

Celia's brow arched. "Did you leave your purse sitting out?"

"No. It's been locked in my closet all day." She panicked, thinking someone might have her house and car keys. "I hate to ask, Celia, but could you give me a lift home and back? I have a set there. If—"

"Sure. No problem." She rested her hand on Jane's shoulder. "I know how bad you must feel. I hate losing things."

"I've never done this before," Jane said, gathering her books. "I feel like I'm losing more than my keys." She pointed to her head.

Celia grinned. "I lost my keys once in the lot of a strip mall. What a mess."

Celia relayed the story as they headed toward the exit. Passing the office, Mary called out and Jane waved goodbye, but before she got outside, Mary called her again.

"I have your car keys," Mary said, flagging her back to the office.

Puzzled, Jane faltered.

"Go ahead," Celia said. "I'll wait."

Jane hurried into the office and Mary pulled the keys out of her desk.

"They were outside most of the day," Mary said.

"Outside? You're kidding."

"Nope. Charlie just brought them in an hour or so ago. You left them in the ignition with the door unlocked. You're lucky someone didn't steal your car."

Lucky? Jane knew better. "Blessed," she said, then realized she hadn't given credit to God in a long time.

Chapter Six

Kyle was naturally suspicious. When Jane told him about the parent who gave her a rough time, he wondered if there might be some connection between Jane's troubles and the man.

When he checked Sam Malik in the police records, he found nothing except a few complaints he lodged against his neighbors. Apparently teachers and neighbors were both on Malik's list.

He'd been anxious to tell Jane what he'd done, and as they sat together in her living room on Thursday evening, he remembered to give her the details.

"Maybe he's tired of complaining and decided to try some action...with me," Jane said, her face strained with tension.

"Could be, but the police need more than speculation."

She crumbled against the sofa. "That's what I can't stand. Nothing can be done until someone threatens me. Or worse." She pulled her back away from the cushion and narrowed her eyes. "When they find my dead body somewhere, then they'll do something.'' Her disheartened sigh filled the air.

He looked at her with his own frustration. "No one's going to hurt you, Jane. I know you're frustrated, but that's the way the law works. The police need hard evidence. At least a suspect."

If he didn't hurt for her—fear for her—his matter-of-fact answer would be exactly that, a fact. But he did care, and he had very little solace to offer her.

As if she'd thought of a new idea, Jane's voice buoyed. "What about the *Dick and Jane* primer?"

Her persistence edged on his own jagged nerves. "I showed you what I found that day at the school when I returned the book. Remember?"

"I guess." She stared down at the floor.

Her downhearted expression tugged at his guilt for being impatient. "All we found was the stamp from the Redmond School District and the name 'Howard' written inside. That's it." He tilted her chin. "And trust me, over the years, many students named Howard went to elementary school in Redmond."

"Did you check?" Her look pierced him.

Kyle flexed his fingers, hoping to relieve his rising frustration. He spoke in a slow, calm voice. "The police department has real crimes to pursue, Jane. They can't spend man-hours searching for crimes that haven't been committed yet."

"That's what I mean. I could be the next real crime," she muttered.

"I know how you must feel, but we need a legitimate threat of harm before we can really act. 'See Jane run' circled on a page isn't it."

Jane flung her arms above her head. "Great. Let's pray for a threat, then."

Though she was driving him up a wall, Kyle wanted to hold her against his chest and comfort her. "Don't be silly. Let's pray that whoever's doing this gets bored with it."

Her head drooped, and she didn't speak for a moment. "I'm sorry, Kyle."

He could see her struggling not to cry.

"I don't want to take my frustration out on you," she continued. "Everything scares me. The other day I turned around and shrieked at my own reflection in the mirror."

She looked so pitiful, Kyle chuckled. "Better that than someone else shrieking when they look at you."

A small grin tugged at the corners of her mouth. "I know. I sound like an idiot."

"No, you sound like a frightened lady who's tired of being afraid." And so was he. He cared too much to see her scared senseless.

Jane studied his face, a combination of tenderness and anxiety. He feared for her. Fear? How many times had Kyle faced fear? Part of the job, she supposed. She'd noticed how he seemed to be alert, standing in just the right way, even when he was off duty. "Are you ever frightened, Kyle?"

Her question seemed to surprise him. "Sure. Why?"

"I don't know. Since this happened I'm jittery all the time. I hear strange noises at night." She ran her fingers over her temples, feeling the beating of her pulse, a throbbing that was too familiar. "I try to push it from my mind, but...I don't know, it seems to overwhelm me."

"Jane, I pray for you every day. But fear shouldn't be part of your job. Fear is built into my job, I suppose. If not fear, anticipation or vigilance. I focus on my weapon and my back, and I guard them both. Redmond is a decent town, so I have it easy compared to some.''

Kyle slid his arm around her, then caught her chin between his thumb and finger. ''Don't worry about me. You have enough to worry about.''

She searched his concerned face, and a new emotion touched her. A different kind of flutter rose in her chest. Not the jackhammer she'd felt of late, this sensation rippled like hummingbird wings. Her breath suspended for a heartbeat.

Kyle's left hand rose, caressing her face. He pressed his palm against her cheek, and his gaze drifted to her eyes, suspended there for a moment, then moved to her lips. His eyes had asked a question, and hers had given the answer. As she tilted her head upward, he lowered his lips to hers.

His fingers slid to the nape of her neck, and pleasure rippled down her spine.

When their lips parted, Kyle's gaze sought hers, his lids heavy and telling. A throaty murmur left him. ''I've been wanting to do that since I met you.'' A long, slow sigh lifted his shoulders.

''So have I,'' Jane admitted quietly. ''Fantasies rarely equal reality, but this time it does.''

''Are you sure?''

''Positive,'' she said.

He looked at her with question, then frowned.

Tangled with concern, she faltered. ''What's wrong?''

''I think we should test these feelings again, just to be certain.''

The tense moment lifted, and a grin curved her lips. ''You have a good point.''

This time they moved in unison, and Jane met his

lips in eager anticipation, exploring the new sensations that raced through her. With her inhibitions abandoned, she lifted her fingers, touching the hollow of his cheek and feeling his stubbled chin. Her hand followed a path to the nape of his neck, drawing her fingers through his thick, toffee-colored hair and cradling his head in her palm.

With tenderness, Kyle drew back and Jane savored the final moments of lips touching lips. Both filled the silence with an audible sigh.

"I'm positive about that kiss being as good as I imagined," Jane said.

"Me, too," he whispered.

She straightened herself in the seat and shifted to face him. "I think I'd better get us something very cold to drink. What do you say?"

"Lots and lots of ice," he agreed.

Kyle stood first, extending his hands to help her rise. She stepped toward the kitchen, and he followed. When Jane opened the refrigerator, Wilcox meandered in and posed nearby. Kyle tousled the cat's fur and gathered him into his arms.

Filling tall glasses with ice first, Jane felt a hidden fear rise up her back. She'd opened herself to Kyle, allowed her heart to admit her growing feelings, but the situation hadn't changed. Though he was dressed like any other man tonight, he often wore a police officer's uniform. Was she setting herself up for hurt?

She brushed the thoughts aside. He was different than her father, she reminded herself. But she had things to think about. Wounds to heal and fears to scatter.

Kyle stood so near she could smell the arousing scent of his aftershave. She poured soda into the glasses, then handed him one. "Now, if you can dump your friend—" she gestured toward the cat "—we can sit and talk about something more pleasant than my problems."

He winked. "Great. What did you have in mind?" He set Wilcox on the floor.

She gave Kyle a gentle poke. "You'd better behave, or I'll tell your father." She walked in front of him to the living room.

"Not that," he teased. "Oh, by the way, my father asked me to invite you to church next Sunday. Sometimes we can get a free dinner out of it."

Her stomach flipped and then righted itself. The first instinct was to find an excuse, but she'd prayed for God's help, and for all she knew, this was God's guidance.

Jane winced, and Kyle sensed her turmoil. "Listen, you don't have to answer me now. Maybe some other time." Though disappointed, he offered the suggestion without reservation.

"Thanks, but I accept." Jane sank into the love seat. "Sorry I didn't answer you right away. It's a long story, but I'm working on some old issues. One of these days I'll overcome them, I hope."

Feeling weighted by her struggle, he slipped into the seat beside her. "Well, church is the best place in the world to lay down your burdens."

Jane laughed. "Are you sure your father wasn't correct? Maybe police work is the wrong career for you. Did you ever think you might be cut out to be a minister?"

"Heaven forbid, and I mean that. I don't have the patience. My father listens without judgment. He's gentle and compassionate. Always has the right words to say to help someone through a problem.''

Jane pressed his cheek with her hand. "That sounds like you.''

Her comment warmed him and brought a smile to his lips. He covered her hand with his. "Now we know what we have to talk about tonight. Reality. I think I'd better tell you about the 'real' me.'' He kept her hand in his, lowering it between them.

"Hmm? This sounds interesting,'' she said.

Once again his heart felt heavy for a moment with the thought of his brother. "My brother should have been the minister. He was gentle and kind, all those things God expects of us. I think that's why he didn't survive the fighting. I'm not sure Paulie could find it in his heart to kill anyone—even in self-defense.''

"I don't believe God expects us to die rather than defend ourselves.'' *An eye for an eye* shot through her mind.

"Me, neither. As hard as Paulie's death was on the family, I think Dad was proud of him for standing up for his belief not to kill. So you see, Dad's not proud that I choose to carry a weapon and even less for being willing to defend myself, even to the point of killing someone.''

His example slammed into her thoughts and jarred her memories. "I can understand how your dad feels, Kyle. When I remember my father going to work, I connect it with violence and death. His pistol frightened me.''

Jane's comment rattled him. Why did some people think of police as symbols of brutality and harshness? Kyle's frustration edged in his voice. "But an officer is more than violence, Jane. What about coming to a person's aid when she needs help? Bringing a lost child home? Safeguarding a person's property against a break and enter. Finding the guilty and prosecuting them? What would the world be without defenders of justice?''

His words jolted her. Instead of the police, God tangled in her thoughts. God did all those things, too, so why did she hesitate accepting the Heavenly Father's help? She only thought of God's wrath, not his compassion and loving kindness.

"You're right. It's easy to forget the good things." Without knowing why, a sense of sorrow inched through her. "I suppose I look at it with different eyes than most."

"I don't know about that," he said.

As he stared into space, the silence weighed heavily on Jane, but she held her tongue.

Finally he looked at her. "So how did you happen to become a teacher?"

The new line of thought surprised her. "I'm not sure. Helping people was important. And I love children. Did a lot of baby-sitting as a girl." Jane wasn't sure why he changed the subject. Though she was relieved, their revelations seemed incomplete. She had so much more she could have said. "Always thought I wanted a big family, lots of kids of my own," she added.

"So? Where are they?"

"Growing up, I changed my mind."

"Why?"

The icy sensation swam through her again. "My mom and dad had a strange marriage. Not very loving. I didn't notice until I was older. Marriage scared me, I suppose."

"Scared or *scares?*" His eyebrows arched, and he leaned forward, waiting for a response.

No sense in lying. "Scares, I guess."

His gaze riveted to hers. "How can you tell if the man you're marrying will be loving and gentle forever?"

"Exactly." She was astounded at his perception. "How does a person know?"

"Trust. Faith. Support. Prayer."

His response caught her unprepared. "I asked my mother why she put up with my dad. What she said shocked me."

Kyle stared at her, obviously expecting an answer, and now that she said it, Jane wished she hadn't brought it up.

"Mom said she loved him, and the good times outweighed the bad." Her heart skipped a beat, remembering that day. "She told me that my dad needed her to keep his balance, and she tempered his behavior with the world. I never knew what that meant."

"Your mom gave him perspective, maybe. Calmed him, let him express his feelings so he could handle them on the job. Something like that."

She contemplated his words, wondering if he were right. "Like if he...lost his temper with her, he'd control it on the job? Is that it?" she asked.

"I don't know, Jane, but I do know that when I visit my folks, they listen to my frustration, my ranting and help me deal with it sometimes. Otherwise, I'd carry on at work and get myself in trouble."

"You?" She tried to picture Kyle angry and out of control. The image didn't form.

"Yes, me. Sure, most people are controlled and professional on the job. They turn the other cheek, bite their tongue, swallow their anger, but when they go home, they slam doors, yell at the kids and kick the cat. They get rid of their frustrations."

His words washed over her. Could it be the truth? Had her father's anger with her mother been only a release from his difficult job? She found the thought too complex to imagine. Yet, how many times had she come home and yelled at Wilcox or slammed a door? Too often to admit.

"I suppose that's true. I have to think about it. I've looked at marriage with a dubious eye, I know."

He slid his arm around her shoulder. "Does this feel dubious to you?"

In feigned modesty, she dropped her chin and twisted her head sideways to peek at him. "No, it feels wonderful."

"I'm sure your mom and dad had those moments, too. Maybe they didn't let you see that part of their relationship."

"Maybe." Her pulsed tripped at the thought. Or was it the look in Kyle's eyes?

Sunday morning, as Kyle parked the car, Jane gazed at the lovely old church. The white clapboard building reminded her of pictures she'd seen of a New England countryside with steeples rising above the autumn-hued treetops. Nearby, confined by a low iron fence, a small cemetery nestled beneath the large oak trees.

"Why is it still so countrified here? I can't believe Detroit hasn't gobbled it up."

"The congregation owns a stretch of woods around the property, so the building and cemetery's protected. I like it here myself."

Kyle climbed out and hurried around the car, but she

swung open the passenger door, not waiting for his chivalry. She grinned apologetically and slid out.

The stone parking lot lay under a blanket of gold and red leaves. Jane shuffled them with her shoe, noticing that the colder evenings had nipped the leaves' edges to a withered brown. But today the sun hung like a golden sphere in the sky, sending a pleasant autumn warmth over her shoulders.

Kyle had gotten them there fifteen minutes early, and the parking lot was partially full already. She noticed the stares when he clasped her hand, nodding at a parishioner as they made their way to the double front door.

As she ascended the church steps, a strange feeling crept up Jane's back. At least three years had passed since she'd been inside a church building, except for her mother's funeral, and she entered feeling ashamed, yet comforted. The ambiguous emotions struggled within her.

Kyle drew her along and ushered her into a pew closer to the front than she wanted to be. Seated in the back, she could readjust to the nuances of a worship service. But she had no choice and settled into the seat as best she could.

To cover her disquiet, she thumbed through the hymn book and glanced at the worship folder, anything to avoid looking at Jesus' eyes staring down at her from the stained-glass windows over the altar.

After a while, the eyes won out. She lifted her face to the scene: Christ, white robed, with his punctured hands extended in welcome. She could hear the words. "Come unto me ye who are weary and heavy laden and I will give you rest."

Kyle was right. If she were ever going to lift the

weight of guilt, this was the only way. She couldn't do it alone. She'd already tried.

Paul Manning came through the side door of the chancel, looking tall and dashing in his pastor's garb. The opening hymn filled her with reassuring nostalgia and the prayers touched her heart.

When Paul rose for the sermon, the man himself impressed her. His words filled the sanctuary, delivered in a rich, compassionate voice.

"And when the Pharisees asked why Jesus and his disciples sat and ate with sinners, Matthew explained to them that only the sick need to visit the physician. As Jesus said, 'I desire mercy, and not sacrifice. For I came not to call the righteous, but sinners.'"

Jane's mind swelled with thought. The truth glowed within her like a rising sun. If she were without sin and shame, she didn't need salvation. But she was ashamed and a sinner, and Jesus was ready to carry her burdens. Her acceptance of the words was the first step. The next step was giving up her load of pain and guilt from so many years.

As the final hymn filled the room, Jane lifted her face again to the stained-glass window. Jesus' eyes rested easily on her now. She prayed in earnest that she would learn to let her burdens go.

Seeking Kyle's profile, Jane drew a long, calming breath. If not for her knight, would she have ever taken a single step toward a new day? She slid her hand along his arm, and his loving look eased away some of the dark, secret anguish in her heart.

After the service, Jane and Kyle waited near the door as Paul greeted the parishioners, and Ruth chatted with passing members. During a lull, Ruth leaned over and whispered in Jane's ear that she hoped the oven timer worked, or the beef roast would never be ready.

The thought of Ruth's roast tugged a faint growl from Jane's stomach, and she pressed her hand against the spot to keep it quiet. For too long, she'd missed home-cooked meals with a family.

With Kyle at her side, Jane stepped into the sun-warmed afternoon. Ruth joined them and the three paused on the sidewalk as Paul locked the building.

Jane's attention shifted to the old graveyard, then to Kyle. "Is your brother buried here or in Arlington?"

Before he could answer, Paul's hand rested on her shoulder. "We wanted him to be close to us."

"That's nice," Jane said, eyeing the gravestones from a distance. "I've always felt comforted wandering through cemeteries, especially old ones. The markers are touching and so interesting."

"Come along," Paul said, taking her arm. "It's a wonderful autumn day to wander."

As he moved her forward, Ruth cautioned him. "Paul, the roast is in the oven. We really should get home."

Paul paused and looked over his shoulder. "Kyle, could you take your mother home? We'll be along shortly."

Jane glanced back and saw a flicker of concern on Kyle's face, but the expression faded as he took his mother's arm. "Okay, but don't occupy my friend all day." He gave Jane a coy wink.

Paul chuckled. "Don't worry. I'll return her safe and sound."

His comment amused Jane. She waved goodbye to Kyle and followed his father toward the wrought-iron fence. As they walked, the dried leaves rustled beneath their feet, and soon, Kyle's car wheels crunched in the stone parking lot as he pulled away. Jane glanced over her shoulder, giving him a final wave.

"Now," Paul said, "let me show you some interesting stones."

"I'd like that. I've never had a guided tour through a cemetery before."

Though her conversation had been easy before, Jane found herself strained, alone with Kyle's father. She longed to talk with him, to look into his compassionate eyes and spill out the worries she'd carried far too long. But she couldn't. What would he think of her?

Paul slowed, then halted. He pointed to a worn marker rising above the ground. "This is one of the oldest."

Jane looked at the inscription dated 1885. "'The Lord is my Shepherd,'" Jane read, looking at the faded sketch of a lamb carved into the stone.

He touched her arm, and she followed him down the grassy path. When he stopped again, Jane studied the markers, all of them telling their own stories.

Ambling along the rows in silence, Jane listened to the natural quiet of the surroundings: singing birds, snapping twigs and chirping crickets.

"Peaceful, isn't it?" Paul said. "Sometimes when I'm thinking through a sermon, I walk here. Our past rises up to meet us, and we're reminded of our finite world and God's gift of eternity." He shook his head. "Amazing."

Jane paused and listened. "This is a peaceful place to think."

"It's so easy to lose sight of what's important. We beat ourselves up for our wrongdoings and our weaknesses. Then I walk here and see that God's given me a full, wonderful life, so I try not to moan about my problems.''

Jane looked at his sincere face as he stood beside her, and she was overwhelmed by awareness about her situation. How much time had she spent in remorse for the past rather than making the most of the present?

''I know Kyle gets upset,'' he continued, guiding her down the path. ''Violence doesn't set well with me. Foolish. I know his work is to preserve order and justice. But I'm his father and frightened for him.''

Jane paused on the grassy path. ''I've spent much of my adult life angry at my father for his career. In my eyes, he was a violent man. Fists and guns. Angry words and loud voices. The memories aren't pleasant.''

''Your dad worked with the vice squad. He had a tough job. But his control always amazed me. Maybe he brought the problems home with him sometimes.''

Jane winced.

''But we all do that, Jane. I try to leave my worries with the Lord, but despite my good efforts, they follow me home sometimes.''

''You? I would think you'd have an easier time dealing with problems.''

''You think I have a special 'in' with the Lord because I'm a pastor?'' Paul rested his hand on her shoulder and chuckled as they moved along. ''No, we all have the same problems—our faith. And we're all sinners, Jane. Me, your dad, you. No matter how hard we try, the human part of us wins out sometimes. Never grieve those moments of weakness. Ask, and you'll be forgiven. Then be strong in the Lord.''

He paused, his eyes downcast. Jane looked near her feet at the flat grave marker. Paul Joseph Manning, Junior.

He crouched down and brushed the leaves away from the stone, his head bowed. Silence hovered on the air.

When Paul rose, he looked at Jane with misty eyes. "I have to listen to my own words, Jane. 'Be strong in the Lord.' Here's where I grow weary. I long to have my son alive though I know he's in a much better place than he could ever find here on earth. Your dad, too."

Jane closed her eyes, hoping Paul was right. "And my mom. She died this summer."

"Well, now, you have had your heartaches." He slid a friendly arm around her shoulder, and they moved along toward the gate. "I suppose Ruth is fit to be tied. The roast will be ruined if we don't get a move on." They picked up their pace, passing the gray granite stones.

For the first time in years, Jane's heart, sometimes as heavy as the grave markers, felt uplifted and hopeful.

Chapter Seven

With apprehension pulsing in his temple, Kyle glanced out the window one more time, wondering what was keeping his dad and Jane. How much sight-seeing could two people do in a cemetery? He cringed, sensing his foolish jealousy. And over his father.

Finally the car pulled into the driveway. When Jane came through the door, she smiled, her hair breeze blown and her color heightened by the outdoors.

"Decided to come back?" he asked his father.

Paul clasped his son's shoulder with a jovial shake. "Couldn't think of anyplace else to go."

He winked at Jane, and Kyle wondered if the wink had some hidden meaning. When his father headed to the kitchen, he asked. "So how was the walk? Okay?" He prayed his father hadn't burdened her with the family concerns again.

"It was nice," she said. "Your dad's a good listener."

He drew back. "What about me?"

"I'd rather do other things than talk when I'm with you."

His concerns eased, and he slid his fingers through hers and led her into the living room. "So what did you talk about?"

"Who do you think you are? The police?" She shook her head.

"Just curious," he said, realizing he'd been pushing her.

But she didn't stop. Jane told him about the old gravestones and his brother's marker, but before she offered details, his mother called them for dinner. It wasn't until he was driving her home that she shared anything significant.

"Your dad gave me food for thought today," she said, her expression concealed by the darkness.

A streetlight lit her face for a moment. Then once again she was in shadow.

He opened his mouth to ask what his father had said, then thought better of it. "That's good."

"He reminded me," she volunteered, "that we spend much of our lives beating ourselves for the past, and in the process, we miss the present." She turned to face him. "He's right, you know."

Kyle nodded, afraid to speak for fear she'd clam up again.

"He reminded me that we only need to ask God for forgiveness, and then move on with our lives. Good advice, huh?"

"Wonderful advice," Kyle said, thanking God and his dad for the wisdom.

She looked out the passenger window, and he wondered what she was thinking. Silence wrapped around them, but thoughts clattered in his head.

The quiet between them made Kyle uneasy, and when he pulled into her driveway, he wondered if he should turn off the ignition or wait for an invitation to come in. He waited.

"Thanks for the nice day, Kyle," she said.

Disappointed, he nodded. "It was nice."

"I know it's still early, but I have some classwork to finish." She dropped back against the headrest. "I dread tomorrow."

Kyle shifted to face her. "Why?"

"Oh, I have to arrange testing for Lena. Skylar hasn't been *too* vocal lately, and I know this will drag his evil looks out of hiding." In the light of her lawn lamp post, he saw her roll her eyes and toss him a wry grin.

Kyle chuckled.

She pushed against the handle, and Kyle jumped out and circled the car to walk her to the door.

"I forgot to tell you," she said, when they reached the porch, "I called my friend Betsy. She's the one married to Perry Jones." She squinted at him. "Remember, I introduced you at the service station the night my tire was flat."

"Right," Kyle said, vaguely recalling the man.

"You should have heard us carrying on when I called. Squeals and nonstop conversation. I'm going to their house Friday night for pizza."

"Friday?"

"You're working, right?"

He nodded.

"I thought our first meeting, after all these years, would bore you. I'd like you to meet them sometime. You can learn more about my past." Teasing, she whispered "past" with an eerie voice.

He laughed. "Hmm? Sounds very interesting." He did his best Boris Karloff imitation.

Jane unlocked the front door, then turned. "Thanks again for the nice day." She touched his arm. "Please don't worry about your folks. I really like them. And I adore your mother's cooking."

"Thanks," he said, sliding his arms around her waist and clasping them behind her. He drew her against him, her small frame dwarfed by his size.

She tilted her lips upward, and he accepted the invitation, this time with an urgency that surprised him. He fought the desire to cave in to his rising emotions and intensify the kiss. Tethering his yearning, he lightened the pressure and savored the softness of her full lips and the sighs exiting her throat.

When he eased back, she shifted a hairbreadth away from him and grinned. "I think it's best that we're saying good-night out here."

"I can't change your mind?" His words were a joke, but his heart longed for her to answer by drawing him into the house.

"Good night," she said, her voice firm and unyielding as if she were talking with her third graders.

He chuckled. "I get the point, Teach. I don't need to sit in the corner."

She stepped through the doorway and closed the storm. He backed down the porch stairs, her delicate body a silhouette against the background light. When he climbed into his car, he drew in a faltering breath. She'd captured his heart. Now all he had to do was prove that she couldn't let her prisoner go free.

Dressed in jeans and a long-sleeve T-shirt, Jane curled up in Betsy's comfy armchair, waiting for her to return from putting the two boys to bed.

"So," Betsy said, moving into the living room, "tell me about this fellow you've been seeing."

Jane stared at the soft drink in her hand, wondering how much she wanted to tell Betsy. Be indifferent, she decided. "Well, the relationship's new. We met when my classroom was vandalized. Then we ran into each other at a restaurant that same evening and he helped put air in my flat tires. That was the night I ran into Perry at the gas station."

"Lucky you, huh?" Betsy said.

Perry came through the doorway and grinned. "She sure was lucky to see me."

"Not you," Betsy said as he plopped beside her. "She was lucky to be rescued again."

"Again?" Jane's mind flew back through their conversation. "Oh, the vandalism. Right. I was glad he was with me." If only they knew how glad, she thought. But Jane didn't want to explain the fears she'd been living with for the past weeks.

Perry gave her a grin. "It's like old times, huh?"

"Sure is," Jane said, remembering so many times in her teen years when the three of them sat together, laughing and eating pizza.

"I meant Kyle," Perry said. "He's like your dad. A cop."

Her smile faltered, but she rustled it up again. "Yes, another cop."

They laughed, and then Betsy returned to her original question. "So tell us about him."

"Not that much more to tell. He's been kind...and fun," she said, filling them in on meeting his parents.

Perry flipped the lever on the recliner and tilted

backward. "I'd hang on to him. He's a nice guy with a good, steady job."

Jane grappled with a response. "Oh, he's great. But the work can be dangerous. I can't help thinking of my dad. You know, the rough, tough cop."

Betsy eyed her. "You felt that way about your dad, Jane. But don't forget, your mom didn't. She loved him. She must've seen a gentler side of him than you."

The truth rang in her comment. "I know, but when I think of Kyle, I always drift back to those difficult days…and a lot of bad memories."

"Sometimes memories are worse than the real thing," Perry said, flipping the footrest down and leaning toward her. "I remember your dad. He never seemed that rough to me."

"Or me," Betsy added. "But we saw him differently, I suppose. I know my parents were always on their best behavior for company."

Jane wondered what she meant. Betsy's folks always seemed friendly and amiable. But then, so had her dad…with company.

Her friends would never know the truth. What bothered her were those private times, under stress, when he pounded his fists and ranted, taking his anger out on her mother. The yelling and foul language still rang in her ears.

Pulling herself from her thoughts, Jane looked into her old friends' expectant faces. "You're probably right. And Kyle is a whole different person. I have to work it out."

The conversation turned to other topics, and Jane finally rose to leave, promising they'd get together soon.

As she pulled away from their house, an urge hit

her. Talking with them had brought the primer to mind. Kyle had studied it, but she hadn't.

Instead of heading home, she decided to drive to the school. A janitor would probably be in the building until his shift ended at eleven. She had a few minutes to stop by and pick up the old textbook. Over the weekend, she'd look through it herself.

A lone car remained in the dark parking lot, and when Jane turned off the motor, her mind shot back to the evening Skylar had surprised her there. Her pulse escalated as she climbed from the car, and she glanced around the shadowy entrance, then steeled herself against her foolish fears.

Despite the words of assurance rolling in her head, she dashed for the back entrance while glancing over her shoulder. When her hand clasped the handle, she was relieved the door was unlocked.

Inside, a strange eeriness settled over her in the familiar surroundings. She'd never had occasion to be in the building alone at night, and in the morgue-like quiet, she peered down the dim hallway before heading for her classroom.

Her rubber soles made a muffled thud in the silence. Amid the hush, a few dimmed lights seemed to hum with electricity. She turned into a darker corridor, and a fearful dread shivered through her. She berated herself for her foolishness.

At her classroom door, she turned the knob. Locked. Good sign. She felt safer. She used the key and stepped inside. To avoid alarming the lone custodian, she ignored the light switch and allowed her eyes to adjust to the dusky room.

The primer was in the bottom drawer, and she darted

to her desk and snatched it out, releasing her pent-up breath. Success.

When she straightened, a shadow covered her as a hand grabbed her arm. Her scream froze in her throat, and her knees buckled when a stick rose above her head.

"No," she yelled, grabbing the desk for support.

The hand released her. "Wh-what are you d-doing here?" The shadowy figure stumbled backward.

Though she recognized her assailant, her body didn't recover as quickly. She clung to the desk for stability, her blood coursing through her veins. "Charlie...what—what are *you* doing?"

In the dim light, his face was as white and frightened as she imagined her own.

"M-Miss Conroy. I—I thought...you we-were... another one of those va-vandals."

"I'm sorry." Giving way to her shaking legs, she sank into her desk chair. "I dropped by to pick up something I'd forgotten. I should have called out."

Clutching the broomstick, he peered at her in the darkness. "S-sure didn't hear you." He gestured toward the door. "And n-no light."

Her quivering hand rested against her constricted chest while the other gripped the book. "I thought I'd be in and out."

Charlie rested his palm on her shoulder, his fingers brushing her hair. She faltered, trying to grasp what he was doing.

He bent over and looked into her face. "Y-you okay?"

She forced a chuckle, flinging her head to one side. Her hair pulled from his grasp. "I think we scared each other, don't you?"

"N-no one could be sc-scared of you. You—you're a pr-pretty lady, M-Miss Conroy." He patted her shoulder, then stepped back.

Her heart pounded. She ached to escape. When she rose, her knees wavered for a moment like sea legs.

With the primer pressed against her chest, he peered at the title.

"D-Dick and Jane." His mouth hung in a loose grin. "That was m-my reading book." He pointed to the cover.

"What?" she said, her pitch rising. "This book is yours?" Fear nailed her to the spot.

"N-not that book," he drawled. "One j-just like it, though."

Innocent? Guilty? Uncontrollable confusion soared through her like seagulls at a picnic. The poor man was as rattled as she was. Taking a step forward to test her quaking knees, she said good-night and tore from the building, leaving Charlie to nurse a case of jitters as absurd as her own.

When she arrived home, her earlier panic etched a ludicrous picture in her mind. She scanned the primer, finding only what Kyle had already mentioned. Weary, she tucked the book in a drawer and climbed into bed.

The next morning, Jane woke and watched the sunlight lay patterns against her bedroom wall. Saturday was her favorite day. She pulled on her robe and went to the kitchen to brew the coffee. Flinging open the back door, the warm Indian summer weather brightened her spirits.

Kyle had suggested a picnic at the Franklin Cider Mill, and Jane thought about what she might bring along. She ate her toast, then carried the coffee cup into the bedroom. She hadn't been to a cider mill in years, and the memory conjured up the aroma of the crushed apples and the sweet taste of the crispy fried doughnuts.

She showered and dressed in jeans, a green and beige knit pullover along with a pair of comfortable walking shoes, hoping she and Kyle would have time to meander along the millstream bank or through the wooded area after lunch.

Looking out at the cloudless sky, Jane pulled out a lightweight jacket, just in case, and headed into the kitchen to prepare some food. Finished, she waited by the front window with her contribution for the picnic, and when Kyle arrived, she scooted out the door.

The Franklin Mill reminded Jane of the Redmond Community Church property. The mill lay nestled in a natural, woodsy glen along a winding stream, not far from the sprawling city. With the warm October sun heavy on the air, the scent of moist earth and pungent aged leaves filled the breeze, and Jane inhaled the aroma as she stepped from the car.

Heading toward the mill, Kyle held her hand, and they followed the stream until the frothing water caught on the mill paddles like strands of iridescent ribbon, then spilled back into the creek in a foaming splash.

The picnic tables were crowded with people nibbling on doughnuts and candy apples. Kyle tucked Jane's hand more firmly in his, and they worked their way to the long line where the heavy scent of apple pulp filled the air.

A bee whizzed past Jane's eyes and tangled in her hair. "Get it out," she yelled, feeling the bee droning near her scalp. She shook her head like a hairy wet dog.

"If you'd quit wiggling, I could," Kyle said, trying to hold her head in place.

She squeezed shut her eyes, and Kyle tugged at her strands of hair as the bee struggled loose and flew away.

He slid his arm around her shoulders. "You shouldn't panic. Bees like sweet places to alight on." He reached up and nuzzled her cheek.

"They scare me to death."

As the words left her, a familiar voice called her name, and Jane swung around.

Celia waved, guiding a tall, trim man toward them.

"Celia," Jane called back, eyeing the good-looking stranger.

"You mentioned the cider mill yesterday, and I suggested it to Len." She gestured to the man at her side. "Len, this is Jane. I've told you so much about her, and this is Kyle." Celia caught the fellow's arm. "This is Len Hirsch."

Len nodded and shook their hands. "Feel like I know you already, Jane. Celia keeps me posted on your exciting life."

"Too exciting for my taste," Jane said. "It's nice to meet you. Now I have a face to go with the name."

Celia glanced behind her at the growing crowd and gave his arm a tug. "Maybe we'll see you later. We need to get in line." With a wave, Celia and Len hurried off.

Jane wiggled her eyebrows at Kyle. "Finally I got to meet the wonderful Len Hirsch."

"He's the new friend?"

"Mmm-hmm," she said as the line moved forward, taking them from the sunlight into the mill.

Inside, the scent of deep-fried doughnuts filled the

room. Her taste buds awakening, Jane remembered the delectable crunchy outer coating of the fried cakes. When they exited the mill, Kyle carried a jug of cider, and Jane, a small bag of crisp, greasy doughnuts.

"Let's find a spot along the stream. You can lay claim while I run back for the picnic basket."

He grabbed her hand, and they followed the stream to a quiet area beneath the trees. Jane sank to the seat, stretching her legs along the bench as Kyle trotted back down the path to the car.

She pulled two plastic cups from her jacket and set them on the table, then poured some cider into one. Taking a long drink, she quenched her thirst with the tangy juice. "This is the life," she said to the trees.

Hearing a bee humming past her ear, Jane ducked and watched it land on the bottle cap. It rose again and buzzed around the cup in her hand. She swished away the pest, then swigged down the cider and turned the used cup upside down on the bottleneck.

The bee droned toward her again.

"Silly bee, go away."

Jane jumped away from the table and wandered along the bank of the stream. Only the hushed sound of the water and an occasional birdcall filled the silence. The noisier crowd at the mill was cut off by the blockade of trees and distance.

A low concrete wall serving as a barricade rose beside a steeper embankment, and she slid onto the rough surface, watching the stream hurry past below her while the pesky bee attacked the cider jug.

With her elbows balanced on her legs, Jane rested her chin on her laced fingers, enjoying the peaceful surroundings. The sunlight shimmered through the trees, dropping diamond sparkles on the swift-running water.

She loved summer, but autumn filled her with a warm, homey feeling, reminding her of bonfire sing-alongs, roasted hot dogs and harvest moons. And now that Kyle had stepped into her life, her days seemed warmer and cozier than they'd ever been.

Hearing the crack of a twig underfoot, Jane glanced over her shoulder. "Kyle?"

She waited, searching for the sign of Kyle or an unseen squirrel, at least. She shot a look up the empty path, then scrutinized the trees and brush. Nothing.

"Kyle? Is that you?" Her silly jitters again. How many times had she jumped at nothing but her imagination? With one last inspection, she turned back to the water.

She wondered what was taking him so long. Tension rose up her neck, and she glanced behind her again. Jane shook her head at her foolishness.

Peering down the stream, she wondered how far she was from the mill and parking lot, but foliage blocked her view. She leaned toward the water, stretched forward and clung to the edge of the concrete, her hands clutching awkwardly behind her.

Kyle's hurried footsteps sounded behind her. "Finally," she said, hoisting herself forward to a safer position on the ledge.

Before she could turn to face him, two hands propelled her forward, and in one black moment, she tumbled from her perch and ricocheted through the tall grass down the jagged embankment.

Chapter Eight

Fear didn't catch up with Jane until she hit the bottom. She skidded down the rocky incline and caught herself against a low scrub bush before skidding into the water. The fall assailed her like a nightmare, and she struggled to face the shocking truth.

Coiled into a protective ball, Jane lay a few feet from the bank, trembling with fear. A throbbing pain shot from her ankle up her leg, and she fought back tears that rushed to her eyes.

Confusion and fright bound her to the hard, cold ground like leg cuffs. Struggling for courage, she looked toward the incline, fearing her enemy would be descending the embankment after her. But she saw no one. The cement ledge and upper bank were empty.

With quivering limbs, she raised herself on hands and knees, testing her throbbing ankle. Hearing sounds above her, she trembled until she detected Kyle's voice.

"Jane?"

She let out a whimpering cry.

"Dear Lord, Jane." She saw him making his way with caution down the steep embankment. "What happened?"

Her tears flowed, and her words were muffled in the hiccuping sobs. He eased her from the ground and wrapped her in his protective arms. She clung against his chest, feeling his heart pounding against her own. Struggling to speak, she opened her mouth again.

"I can't understand you." He bent his ear toward her face. "Are you hurt? What happened?"

She tugged the words from her throat. "Someone pushed me."

"Pushed you?" He eyed the embankment. "Who? Did you see who it was?"

She shook her head, unable to speak.

"Are you hurt?"

She pushed back the welling tears. The pain knifed into her foot. "Just my ankle."

He crouched and pulled up her pant leg, inspecting her ankle while she braced herself against his back. His fingers gently probed the lower leg and ankle bone, and she flinched with his cautious touch.

Voices sounded above them, and Jane jerked her head upward. "What happened?" Celia leaned over the cement wall, her eyes wide. Len stood beside her.

"She took a tumble," Kyle called. "I'll explain later."

He straightened her jeans, then stood and captured her shoulders in his hands. "I'm sorry I took so long. I invited Celia and Len to join us, and I waited to show them the way. I'm so sorry."

"You didn't know." She looked into his eyes through a blur of tears. "And neither did I, or I wouldn't have turned my back." She thought of him, the way he was always on guard.

"Can you put weight on your ankle?"

"I'll try." When she lowered her foot flat on the ground, the throbbing increased up her leg.

Kyle slid an arm around her supporting her weight at the shoulder, then looked up the embankment. "Len, can you come down and give us a hand? I'd like to keep pressure off this ankle."

Len grabbed the rough ledge for balance, then turned and edged down the incline sideways. "How'd you fall?" he asked as he neared the bottom.

Jane shivered. "Someone pushed me off that ledge."

He scowled. "Someone what?" His voice rose in disbelief. "Kids, huh?"

"I didn't see who it was." Tears pressed against the back of her eyes, and she squeezed her lids closed, controlling the torrent that struggled for release.

"Grab her under the other arm like I'm doing," Kyle instructed. "We can keep some of the pressure off the foot."

Jane stared up the steep embankment, wondering how they would keep from tumbling back down again. But they supported her arms and eased her off the ground, keeping her weight from the ankle. They pressed forward, stepped, then paused, until they reached the top.

As soon as they set her down, Celia threw her arms around Jane's neck. "It's terrible. When will it end?"

"I wish I knew," Jane murmured, still unbelieving.

As if on the job, Kyle took charge. "Could you grab the stuff—the cider and cooler—while I get her to the car?"

Celia and Len responded and gathered the gear while Kyle shouldered Jane to the parking lot.

Before reaching Kyle's car, Len stopped and motioned to his. "Mine's right here. I'll throw your stuff inside, and we'll follow you. Hospital or where?"

Jane stiffened at the word *hospital*. "No, I'll be fine. Let's go to the house. If something's really wrong, I promise I'll go then. I want to get out of these dirty clothes, and—"

"And you want your doughnut," he said, maneuvering her into the seat.

She could only nod, trying to change her grimace to a grin. He closed the door, and Jane rested her head against the seat back. When they were on the highway heading home, Jane related the whole story, beginning with the cider and the irritating bee.

After she finished her tale, Kyle remained silent. His hands gripped the steering wheel, and she figured he was concluding what she was. "I'd like to think this is a coincidence, Jane, but…"

"I know. The thought's been going through my mind. But why? What have I done to cause someone so much hatred? Even in my past, I can't imagine anything."

"Don't look for anything sensible. What happened before you were pushed?"

Recalling the moment, her chest tightened. "I thought it was you. From the footsteps." Visions she didn't want to imagine crashed through her mind.

Kyle stared at the road. "Size? Any impression? Could it have been a woman?"

A woman? Celia? Was she a suspect? Impossible. "No, not a woman. The person was too strong. The footsteps too heavy."

"Heavy because the person was running? A man or woman hitting you with a running force could jettison you over the edge without a problem."

"Maybe, but...."

Kyle's line of questioning faded. "I'm just brainstorming, Jane."

"Be honest, Kyle. Are you thinking it's Celia? I can't believe that."

He glanced at her. "Not really. I'd been talking to her minutes earlier, but she knows your comings and goings."

"Impossible. And she has no motive." Confusion addled her thinking. "No. Absolutely not."

"How about her friend?"

"Len? I don't even know him. I met him today. Anyway, you were with him, you said."

"I was, until he ran their cider to the car." He shook his head. "Forget it. I'm a cop, Jane. Everyone's a suspect. It could be anyone."

She shifted in the seat, lifting her foot higher on the car floor and hoping to relieve some of the throbbing.

Kyle eyed her movement. "Foot hurt?"

She told another of her whopping untruths. "Just a little." If she didn't hurt so badly, his tender expression would have touched her, but she could barely think.

"Do you have one of those elastic wraps at home? I want to wrap your ankle."

"I don't know." Jane forced herself to focus on bandages. "No, I don't think so." Instead of thinking of foot wrappings, her thoughts were jumping from Skylar to Celia, then to Len and Sam Malik. Finally, to Charlie.

For a moment, even Kyle was suspect. She released

a jagged breath, forcing away the tears that pressed behind her eyes.

"Pain?" Kyle asked, his face etched with worry.

"Everything," she said, wondering when it might end. She shifted her head against the headrest. Should she admit to Kyle that he could be a suspect, too? She had to think things through. Set traps?

Laughter and tears pervaded her at the same time. Traps? How could she think such a thing. Kyle's father was a pastor. But hadn't Kyle said he wasn't like his father? Her nails dug into her clenched fists. She unwound her fingers, stretching them in her lap.

"When we get to your place, I'll get some ice on your ankle, and then I'll run out and pick up an elastic bandage. That should help. If it's a break, I'll take you to Emergency."

"It's not that bad, Kyle. I can see my doctor on Monday."

"I know the difference between a sprain and a break. Boys in blue are ready for everything. We help little ol' ladies across the road, we deliver babies and we catch criminals. We can even bandage a sprain."

Studying his concerned profile, Jane dismissed her suspect thoughts. Kyle cared about her.

She looked out the window and was grateful they were nearly home. Kyle pulled into the driveway, and Len parked behind him. As they hurried from the car, Kyle apologized. "I'll need to get out, Len. After I get Jane inside, I want to pick up an elastic wrap for her."

Len glanced at his car. "Look, I'm parked behind you. Let me go. I saw a pharmacy right up the road. You and Celia can get Jane inside."

The decision made, Len pulled away while Kyle scooped Jane into his arms and headed for the porch.

He lifted her as easily as a child, and she felt like one cradled lovingly in his arms.

"Door key?" He braced her weight against his knee.

"In my…" Concern smacked her. "Did someone pick up my purse?"

"Sure did," Celia said, then grimaced. "All the stuff's in Len's car."

"So we wait," Kyle said with a look of distress.

Jane hesitated. She kept a key hidden outside for such occasions, but distrust bogged her disclosure. Could Celia or Kyle…? Her heart answered her question.

"Problem solved," Jane said. "I have a house key in one of those fake rocks under the shrubs there." She gestured to the landscaping beneath her front picture window. "It looks real but the bottom slides."

Celia stooped down and, in a moment, pulled out the artificial rock. "This? It's the biggest one here."

"Looks like it," Jane said.

Celia turned the stonelike object over and slid the back away. "Voilà," she said, exposing the key.

Celia unlocked the door, and by the time Len returned, Jane was sitting with her foot propped on a stool, her ankle packed with ice.

Wilcox sauntered up to Len with a plaintive meow.

"Who's your friend?" Len asked, handing Kyle the pharmacy bag. He bent down and nuzzled the cat's fur.

"Wilcox," Jane said, feeling relief from the numbing ice. "He thinks he's family."

Len gave her a knowing nod. "Family is family." He grinned at her ice-weighted ankle. "How does it feel?"

"Better."

"Good." He took a step toward the doorway. "I'll get the rest of your stuff, and then Celia and I'll leave you guys alone."

Kyle dropped his hand on Len's shoulder. "Don't run off. We still have a picnic."

Celia moved to Len's side. "No, Jane's been through enough. We'll bring the stuff in and be on our way."

"Appreciate your help," Jane said from the confines of her chair.

"That's what friends are for," Celia said with the shake of her head. "Sorry things turned out this way."

When the supplies were inside and they'd gone, Kyle fixed Jane a sandwich and poured her a glass of cider.

Though she'd felt hungry earlier, Jane's appetite had faded. She nibbled on a crust, feeling helpless.

Kyle had no problem. While he chomped on his three-decker concoction, she watched him, grateful for his friendship. In the past weeks, she'd grown to care about him more than she wanted to admit. Her restless nights were filled with memories of their first cautious kiss.

Now it was different. He slipped his arm around her with natural ease, and often his eyes sought hers, filled with a look that melted her heart.

Motivated by memories, she'd struggled to control her feelings, but she was losing the battle. Though she'd made a promise long ago to steer clear of cops, when she met Kyle, she'd broken the promise.

His face filled with question, Kyle broke the silence. "What's on your mind?"

She faltered, knowing how he always knew her thoughts. "Just thinking," she said.

"Me, too. I want you to get a cell phone. Everyone has them…and right now, you need one."

Her spirit lifted at his concern. "Good idea. I suppose I'm old-fashioned not owning one."

"You said it." He gave her a toying wink, then clamped his mouth around the last bite of sandwich.

Her thought slipped back to the cider mill. "I'd thought today would be so different." She felt embarrassed now at her earlier romantic visions. She'd pictured them nestled on a bench, eating doughnuts and—

"Me, too. In more ways than one," he said, reaching across the table to capture her hand.

His touch surprised her. "What do you mean?" she asked, but praying he'd say what she'd been thinking.

Amusement curved his lips. "Better yet, I'll demonstrate."

"Demonstrate?" Her heart swelled, recognizing his familiar prattle.

He rose, bracing his weight on the chair arms and lowered his lips to hers.

Jane met his mouth. Yielding to his tenderness, she lingered there before drawing away.

"Well?" Kyle asked, hovering above her, their lips so near, she could feel his breath brush against her skin. "We may get that right with practice."

Pleasure rippled down Jane's spine.

Kyle straightened his back. "Not quite the way I'd imagined it, but very nice all the same. So now, how about a greasy doughnut?"

"Why not?" she said, savoring the taste of his lips above her long-awaited fried cake.

He tugged open the grease-soaked bag and reached inside. A scrap of paper came out with the doughnut. Kyle hesitated, then unfolded it, scanned the message and handed it to Jane. His face told the story.

Tears filled her eyes and ran down her cheeks. When she saw the words, the horror cut through her heart. *Look! Look! Look! See Jane fall.*

Chapter Nine

By Monday when she returned to school, Jane's sprained ankle was only slightly swollen. When Lena came through the door, Jane heard news that froze her to the spot.

"Miss Conroy, did you see me at the cider mill?"

Jane's heart skipped a beat. "No, Lena. Were you there?"

"Yep, my daddy took the whole family to buy cider."

Jane wanted to quiz the child for more details, but cautioned herself. A coincidence. That's all it was.

"I wanted to watch the waterwheel and say hi to you, but Daddy made us sit in the car while he talked to a friend."

Jane struggled to keep her voice calm. "Maybe next time," she said, her pulse racing. Sam Malik went to talk to someone? Could it be he went to *push* someone? She couldn't allow herself to think about it. She remembered her plan to lay her burdens on Jesus, but they clung to her, and the fear chilled her to the bone.

*   *   *

As soon as Jane saw Kyle, she told him about Malik being at the mill. But as always, the police could do nothing. Kyle warned her to stay rational. His attitude jolted her with disappointment.

Frustrated, Jane's mind whirled. If the police would do nothing, she would do something. She pulled out a note-pad and listed everyone she knew who'd been at the cider mill. Kyle, Celia, Len—and now Sam Malik. Had it been one of them? Or someone lurking in the shadows? Kyle and Celia? Never. Weighted with shame, she rested her chin on her folded hands and thought.

By Wednesday, her ankle seemed almost back to normal, and she pushed the fear as far from her as she could. At school that morning, heading for her teacher's mailbox, Mary handed her a note.

Jane glanced at the memo, and her heart sank. She had another meeting after school with Mr. Malik. Then, remembering Skylar's instructions, she caught Mary's attention.

"Would you ask Mr. Skylar to sit in on my parent conference this afternoon? Mr. Malik is coming in to go over Lena's test results, and Mr. Skylar suggested he should be there." Suggested? He'd demanded.

Mary's brows knit together. "He isn't in today, Jane. He's at a two-day conference."

Two days? "Postpone the meeting then."

Mary shrugged. "That's up to you. The man sounded rather adamant that he meet with you today."

"What do you think I should do, Mary?"

She shook her head. "It's up to you."

Jane dealt with the problem. She used the conference phone and called Sam Malik, but nothing would change his mind. He insisted meeting with her after school. When she replaced the receiver, she folded her hands and prayed.

Heading to the classroom, she felt burdened with too many problems. Tonight, Malik, and tomorrow, a meeting with her co-workers that could prove difficult.

With Halloween approaching, Jane, along with other teachers who opposed the school's traditional celebrations, agreed to discuss an alternative activity, something special for the classes. She prayed that most of the teachers would agree to find a more acceptable way for the students to celebrate the harvest.

Morning class plodded along, and at noon, Jane gulped her lunch and spoke with Betty Durham, the special education teacher. After they reviewed the test for the second time, Betty offered to sit in with Malik, but knowing Malik's attitude, Jane refused.

At the end of the day, Jane took a deep breath and met with him, despite Skylar's orders. She covered the test scores point by point. When she finished, he leaned back against the chair and sneered.

"I expected as much," he said. "I know my daughter. No matter what you say, she's slow and needs help. If you can't provide my daughter with a proper education, you'll hear from my lawyer."

"But, Mr. Malik, I really—"

"No 'buts' about it, Miss Conroy. You and I'll be sitting in court."

He rose and stalked from the room.

The second weekend after Jane's fall, Kyle lounged in her living room, watching her pull a piece of pepperoni from the top of a double-cheese pizza. He studied her slender fingers as she plucked the round disk from the mozzarella, raised it to her mouth, then dropped it between her lips.

He couldn't keep his attention away from her soft, pliant mouth, longing to kiss her. Somehow she kept her emotions in check like a bulldog. He admired that.

Unsuccessfully he'd tried to do the same. Their kisses had been few, considering how eager he was to lavish her with them. And often he wondered if he were protecting her or himself.

Being a cop made falling in love dangerous. How many times had an officer been shot down, trying to avoid gunfire...thinking about his wife and kids? Wife. He let his gaze explore every inch of Jane's slender frame.

"Why are you staring at me?" She licked her messy fingers. "Suppose you think I'll drop over from high cholesterol."

Her look sent waves of emotions charging through him. "No, I was wondering what it might be like to be that pizza."

"Huh?" Her nose wrinkled.

His heart skipped a beat with his developing plan. "I'll show you." He rose from the chair and moved to the sofa, slipping his arm behind her as he settled.

Her expressive eyes followed him in question.

"See, I'll be that piece of pizza. Now...you do your part." He leaned toward her, and she did exactly as he requested.

She met his mouth eagerly, savoring the first taste, then nibbled his lower lip, teasing, lingering for a moment before she covered his mouth again.

When he thought he might die, she drew back to catch her breath.

"Whew!" he said, looking into her laughing eyes.

"Now that was some pizza. But I should mention I always have more than one slice."

She braced both palms against his chest. "Not this pizza you don't. But here you go." She snatched a slice of the real thing and raised an edge to his lips while she nipped at the other end.

He licked the sauce from his mouth and protested, "Delicious, but not fair."

"Not fair, but safer."

Wilcox rose from his curled fur ball and slithered over to Jane's feet, wrapping himself around her ankles.

Kyle gestured to the cat. "See. There's someone who won't settle for wishful thinking. He wants food."

"I'm not worried about the cat," she said. "Just about you."

Wondering how long he could hang on, he took a deep breath and prayed. He cared about her too much to let anything jeopardize their growing relationship.

Jane nuzzled her head against his shoulder. "I feel safe when you're here, Kyle. I'm so jittery. I jump at every sound. But it's been quiet for a couple of weeks. I don't know if it's over or just a welcomed lull."

She looked at him with fearful eyes, and he ached for her. "If I could do something, I would. Not just me, but the department."

"I know, there's nothing concrete. You told me that. Everything could be accidental."

"Not anymore, Jane. Now, we have the notes on file. They dusted, but no fingerprints. Still, if something clicks to give us a clue to the perpetrator, we can build a case and file charges. But we need a suspect. Any thoughts? That art teacher, Larry, or the teacher you replaced, Dale Keys?"

"It doesn't make sense. Why would they want to hurt me?" She shook her head. "But I'm keeping notes."

"That's good. You're probably right, Jane, but please, don't play detective." Kyle drew his finger down her jaw to her lips. "Are things better at school?"

"Not really. Since the Malik situation, Skylar's giving me those pursed-lip expressions." She shifted to face him. "Did I tell you that our meeting about the autumn celebration went well?"

"Autumn celebration? What's that?"

"An activity to replace the Halloween party. Being a Christian, I don't like the witch and goblin thing. So I talked it up at the meeting, and we decided to have a harvest celebration."

He admired her courage. Like his brother, Paulie, she wasn't afraid to stand up for her beliefs. "What will you do?"

"We're going to a pumpkin farm. After a hayride and farm tour, they help the children paint pumpkins. The workers even dress like scarecrows."

"That sounds fun. I'm proud of you for standing up for your beliefs."

"You are?"

He nodded, then raised his hand and caressed her hair, feeling the mass of curls beneath his fingers. Although unwanted, his mind drifted back to the stalker situation. "Jane, we still need to come up with a suspect. Are you thinking about people you know...or people you knew years ago who might be involved in this?"

"I don't know. I've asked myself a million questions

about everyone, Kyle.'' She lowered her head, and a faint flush rose on her cheeks.

''And?'' He could guess what she was thinking.

''I've even wondered about you.''

As she lifted her head, he saw her eyes filled with sadness, and he hurt for her.

She shook her head. ''I can't believe it. But once in a while, I remind myself that you've been nearby during most of the incidents.''

''I suppose I have. The tires, the notes, the book.''

''And at the cider mill,'' she added.

How could he blame her? He could be as guilty as anyone.

Jane pulled her hand through her curls. ''I even wondered about Celia after you mentioned the guilty person could be a woman. But in my heart, I know it's neither of you.''

Kyle wished he could do something to ease her fears. He slid his arm around her shoulders. ''I don't blame you for wondering, Jane. I keep wishing something might trigger your memory. Someone who was jealous of you in your past. Someone who wants revenge. Maybe you were a beauty queen and stole the crown from a 'wanna-be'?''

''I wasn't a cheerleader or the queen of anything. I told you. I've gone over it so many times. I even asked my friends Perry and Betsy.''

''Nothing, huh?''

''Nothing. They both agree I'm purely delightful.''

Her flickering grin caused him to smile. ''Well, then. We'll wait and see.''

''I don't want to hear 'wait and see' anymore.'' She raised her finger and traced the line of his mouth.

His stomach tightened, and he wondered what she was thinking as he studied her serious expression.

"Kyle," she said finally, "you're wonderful. Handsome and brave and...I—I don't understand."

Her look put him on edge so he went for humor. "You don't understand why I'm wonderful, handsome and brave?"

"No, why you're single. Why you haven't married. You could have a girl on every corner."

"What makes you think I don't?" he joked, but her question was a direct hit.

"You always make a joke when I ask you something serious," she said. She stared at him, waiting for a response.

How could he answer her? It was a feeling more than anything else. Families hurt when loved ones died. He knew the pain himself. Marriage and cops? He wasn't sure the two went hand in hand.

As he searched for an answer, Jane studied him.

"I scare women off with my wonderfulness. Do you believe that?"

"Kyle, that's another joke. Please."

He owed her this one, no matter how difficult it was to explain. "Family, maybe. I value families, and I've watched my parents' pain...and felt my own when Paulie died. His death blasted a hole in my family as horrible as the bullet that put a hole in him."

A long time had passed since Kyle dealt with these feelings. The pain swelled in him like a sucker punch.

Jane seemed to sense his distress. Caressing the back of his hand, she didn't speak, but her face said she understood.

"When I leave for work in the morning," Kyle continued, "I never know if I'll come home at night. I've asked myself many times if I want to put the woman I love, maybe even kids, through that kind of agony. You've lived it, Jane. You told me. You understand.''

Her head drooped. ''Then…what about us?''

His serious words were cushioned with a comfortable awareness. ''Emotions don't seem to use reason. They just grow into relationships. I can't fight it anymore, Jane. Like the old song says, 'Whatever will be, will be.' ''

Her stressed face softened to a smile. She lifted her empty fingers, pinched them together as if holding something, and waved them back and forth. ''Can you tell what's in my hand?''

''You're directing a band?''

''It's my white flag. I surrender,'' she said with a shy look Kyle had never seen before.

For a moment, he lingered on her smile. When he leaned forward to kiss her, she wrapped her arms around his neck, and he could feel her hand waving the imaginary flag above his head.

Chapter Ten

On Wednesday of the next week, Jane stopped at a neighborhood café for dinner before she returned to school for her first parent open house. Though Kyle was working the afternoon shift, he said he'd try to join her, and she grinned when she saw him come through the door.

"Things are quiet tonight," he said, sliding into a chair across from her. "I called in my dinner break. They'll radio me if there's a problem."

"I'm glad. I miss you on this shift."

He slid his hand over hers. "I miss you, too." His seasoned eye studied her face. "Something wrong?"

Lying to him made no sense. He could read every nuance of her expression. "A little nervous, I suppose. This is my first parent open house. I'm not sure what to expect."

"Thinking all your parents will be like Malik?"

"Something like that." She glanced again at the menu, then laid it next to her place setting. "My room looks nice though."

"Anything special?"

"I've put up all the science and social studies projects. The drawings of Michigan birds and flowers are pretty. And then we made a fort out of Popsicle sticks. Not bad if I do say so myself."

"Wish I'd had a third grade teacher like you."

Before she could respond, the waitress stopped by to take their order.

When she left, Kyle gripped her hand more tightly. "Okay, now it's my turn."

His face appeared relaxed, but his words frightened her. "Is something wrong?"

"Not really."

He was lying. She saw it in his face. Her pulse skipped. "Is it something about me?"

He didn't respond, but she saw a teasing glint in his eyes.

"Come on, Kyle."

"It's about *us,* but I'm not sure you're ready to hear this."

"Say it." She shook her hand captured beneath his. "You're driving me crazy."

"That's it, Jane. You're driving *me* crazy. You're all I think about."

Her galloping pulse became a stampede of wild horses, but she struggled to keep some focus on reality. No matter how much he made her heart skip, he was a cop. "But we've only known each other such a short time."

He lifted her hand to his lips and brushed it with a kiss. "It's been less than two months, I know. But is time really that important?"

"It's not just time." She eyed his familiar blue uniform, the badge, the weapon. Memories and fear sailed into her mind. It was too much too soon. "Since I met you, I've been under so much pressure. And...my dad, well, I have a lot of negative feelings about—"

"I'm not your dad, Jane. And I'm not pushing you for anything right now. I just want you to know what I'm feeling."

"Then I'll be honest. You're important to me, too." But was important enough? Would time soften the excitement and fade into bad feelings and resentment— old hurts resurfacing?

He nestled her hand between his. "Just remember."

"How can I forget?"

But Jane sensed he had something more serious on his mind. "What else, Kyle? You're thinking again about something."

He studied her. "I'm thinking about your past, Jane. Does anyone you work with seem familiar—someone you knew years ago? Skylar? Charlie, maybe? Or how about Dale Keys?"

Irritation surged up her spine. "You're stuck on this *past* thing, Kyle." She flung her hands out to her sides. "I recognized Perry right away. People change, but not that much."

"I'm sorry for pushing you, Jane, but...forget it. Don't worry about it."

Though his expression looked apologetic, she glowered at him. "*Don't worry?* Easy for you to say." Immediately she was sorry.

"You carrying the cell phone?" he asked.

She nodded, recalling the black compact telephone in her shoulder bag, which should be giving her a sense of safety. But it didn't.

Kyle became thoughtful. Jane looked at the concern on his face and wanted to reach out and hug him...kiss him for his goodness. He'd done everything he could, and she acted so ungrateful.

The day they met rose in Jane's mind. She remembered how his uniform caused a gate as thick as a castle wall to drop between them. But Kyle's gentleness and good humor punched holes in the barricade she'd built. Little by little it was crumbling away.

Still, at times, the memories rose, tearing at her like a wild circus lion, and she would hold them back with the whip of reason and sensibility. Then the lion transformed to a kitten again, purring against her chest, becoming her best friend.

Jane refocused as the waitress appeared and slid the platter of pesto pasta in front of her, its savory aroma tempting her appetite. Tonight she'd appease her stomach. If she could only do the same for her thoughts.

Before the parents arrived for the conference, Jane organized her displays and set out students' math workbooks. She jumped when Celia leaned into the room. "Can you do me a favor?"

Jane chastised herself for her jitters. "Sure. What?"

"Unlock my door."

Unlock her door?

"I left the key at home in the blazer I wore yesterday."

"You mean my key opens your classroom?" Jane asked.

She nodded. "All the keys in this hall are the same. All the corridors are that way."

Jane's mind grasped the new piece of information, tucking it in her mental file; then she followed Celia. When she reached the hall, Charlie stood outside Celia's room.

"Never mind, Jane," Celia said. "Charlie'll do it."

Jane nodded and watched Charlie unlock the door. He attached the key to the ring on his belt while his gaze fastened on Jane.

An eerie feeling crept over her. She wet her dried lips and hurried back into her classroom. Her first parent entered on her heels.

Trying to spread herself between the parents who arrived, Jane used all the tact she could muster. The hardest part of the evening was dismissing parents who didn't want to stop talking.

Her feet ached, and her mind muddied as the last few parents wandered around the room, viewing their children's work. To Jane's relief, Sam Malik didn't appear, and her tension faded as time moved forward.

At nine o'clock, the P.A. hissed, and Skylar's voice concluded the evening with a "thank you" to the parents and an announcement ending the open house.

Jane spent the next few minutes edging parents toward the doorway. As the last couple made their way through the exit, she closed her door with a deep exhale.

Though she felt tired, the evening lifted her spirits. Her students liked her, that was certain. She heard it in the parents' voices. She closed the workbooks, placed them on the shelf, then slipped on her coat and locked her room.

Heading for the exit, Jane slowed her pace. An old fear slithered into her mind. The parking lot set her imagination whirling.

As she opened the wide outside door, Celia caught up with her. Having company, Jane relaxed. They compared notes on the open house, and as Jane approached her car, she pushed the keyless remote and heard the comforting beep. Celia said good night and moved off toward her own car.

Jane started the motor before she noticed something under her windshield wiper. Her breath shallowed, and she slammed her eyelids closed, praying it was only an illusion or shadow. Opening them, she caught her breath. It was really there.

Peering cautiously into the shadows, she steeled herself and threw open the door. In a matter of seconds, she'd grabbed the paper, hopped back into the car and pushed the lock button.

She sat like a statue, staring at the folded paper. Celia's headlights retreated from the parking lot. Jane wanted to laugh at herself. Maybe it was only a note from Kyle saying he'd drop by later…or a scribbled thank-you from an appreciative parent.

She inched open the paper and squinted into the darkness. In the dashboard light, she saw three printed words. Her heart rose to her throat.

She tilted the paper closer to the dash. *See Puff vanish.* The words made no sense, but the pattern was the same as the others.

Her immediate thought was Kyle. She opened her purse, and gratitude filled her mind as she dug inside for the phone. How would she feel now if she hadn't heeded Kyle's advice? Staring at the push buttons, she had second thoughts. Why not just drive to the station?

She peered through the windows, watching cars file from the parking lot. She was nearly alone. She dropped the phone to the passenger seat and shifted into reverse. She'd feel better in a lighted building than alone in a dark parking lot.

In a few minutes, Jane arrived at the precinct and hurried into the building, wondering what to say. How could she explain that a note saying "See Puff vanish" frightened her? She prayed Kyle was there.

As she approached the desk, a woman in uniform rose and met her at the counter.

"Can I help you?" she asked

"Kyle Manning? Is he around?"

"No, he's out. Would you like to talk to another officer?"

Jane's spirit nose-dived. "Not really. He's my...well, a friend, and I thought maybe—"

The woman's face broke into a broad smile. "Are you Jane?"

"Yes." Relief. The tension fell from her shoulders. "I need to talk with him, but it can wait."

"I can call him and see where he is."

Her pulse skipped. "Could you? Thanks."

Jane listened to the static-filled squawk of the radio, trying to make sense out of the noise.

"Can he meet you at your house?" the officer asked.

"That would be great."

The woman repeated her message and ended the call. She gave her a smile. "He'll pass by your house."

Jane thanked her, then hurried to her car and home. As soon as she arrived, Kyle's squad car lighted the road from the opposite direction. He pulled in behind her.

Kyle exited the squad car, his broad chest and towering frame a refuge for Jane. The sensation charged through her. Instead of fear, she felt safe, seeing the blue uniform.

Silhouetted in the front seat, Jane noticed another figure. She felt embarrassed to share her silly fears with a stranger.

She stepped from the car and met him on the grass.

"What's wrong?" he asked, his voice deep with worry.

Her hands trembling, Jane handed him the note.

He used his flashlight to see the words. "What does it mean?"

"I don't know." She stared at the small paper in his large hand.

"It's like the other messages...except what's a puff?"

Jane shrugged.

He glanced toward the squad car. "Let me see if George has any ideas." He walked back to the other officer.

Though the note was meaningless, the cryptic message frightened her. Puff. She faltered. Was that the Dick and Jane cat? She braced herself against the car to combat the horrible sinking feeling.

The second officer followed Kyle from the car and introduced himself. "Puff's the cat in *Dick and Jane*," George said, validating her own thinking. "You don't happen to own a cat, do you?"

She nodded, her heart hammering double time.

"We'd better take a look," Kyle said. He clutched Jane's arm and steered her toward the doorway.

Stunned and fearful, she let Kyle lead her up the porch stairs and turn the door handle. "It's locked, Jane."

Hope filled her. If her tormentor couldn't get inside, Wilcox was safe. She handed Kyle the key. He entered first.

Jane flipped on the light switch. She faltered. Wilcox usually greeted her at the door. She raced through the house, calling the cat's name. Wilcox was silent. A wave of nausea swept through her.

"Do you see anything missing?" Kyle asked, surveying the rooms as they passed through.

"Just Wilcox," she said, her legs weakening with each step.

George returned from the kitchen. "The back door's locked. It looks like a hoax."

Jane stopped in the hallway. "Maybe, but where's my cat?" She dashed into her bedroom with the men behind her. Pivoting, Jane saw nothing out of place. But before she spoke, an urgent "meow" came from her closet. She froze.

Kyle's hand shot forward, pushing her out of danger, and he edged toward the closet, his pistol drawn. Then, stepping to the side, he yanked open the door.

Wilcox leaped from the confines and darted from the bedroom with George hurrying after the cat.

Dazed, Jane gaped at the action.

"You must've locked him inside when you got dressed this morning," Kyle said, eyeing the closet.

"I don't think so. If I did, what about the note? Is that another coincidence?"

A ragged sigh escaped him. "Jane, I don't know."

Her hands knotted to fists. "And who knows I have a cat? That scares me, Kyle."

Seeming distracted, Kyle gave her a faint nod, then crouched in front of the closet and frisked the floor. Palming something, he straightened and gave her an uneasy look.

George barreled through the doorway. "The cat seems to be okay," he said, cradling Wilcox in his arms. He came to a stop.

Kyle glanced at him, then back to the slip of paper clutched in his fingers. He unfolded the note and scanned the message, then shook his head. He thrust the paper in Jane's hand.

She stared at the words. *See Jane suffer.* Tears she'd struggled to control streamed down her cheeks, and she swung toward Kyle. "I can't stand this anymore."

He wrapped his arms around her, drawing her against his chest, and she gave the sobs free reign. When she calmed, she lifted her head. "How did he get in? The doors were locked...."

Suddenly the answer struck her. She bolted from his arms and down the hallway. The key in the rock. Someone knew. But who? Celia...and Kyle...or Len. No, he'd been at the pharmacy. Or had Celia told him about the key? Maybe someone else had stood in the bushes and watched her.

Kyle tensed when she broke loose and darted from the room. With George on his heels, he followed, having no idea where she was headed until he saw her open the front door. Then he remembered the key. He stood at the door as she knelt on the ground, groping beneath the shrubs.

He jumped off the edge of the porch as she pulled out the rock. The key lay inside, as if untouched. She raised her face to his, tearstains lacing her ashen skin.

"It's here. Would a burglar put it back?"

"Maybe, Jane. The person is obviously playing games." He drew her from the ground, his heart heavy. The bottom of her skirt was wet from the damp earth. He was overwhelmed with sadness...and anger.

He clutched her against his chest, his wary eyes scanning the shrubbery and street. Was someone in the dark watching now? Who was getting a sick delight out of scaring her to death? And why?

A sound caused him to reel toward the porch.

George stood in the doorway holding open the storm door. "What's up? Find anything?"

He shook his head, "She keeps a key here." He showed George the rock. "But it's still inside. I wouldn't think anyone would put it back."

George shrugged. "I'll call the station and see if they want to dust for fingerprints. What do you say?"

"Good idea."

His mind was more torn than it had ever been. With Jane involved, he wasn't thinking clearly. And he needed to be on his toes. The old fear knifed through him. Marriage and cops? The two didn't mix at all.

He pushed the thought out of his head. He had to go over the whole thing step by step with Jane. What were they missing? A person didn't stalk someone without a reason. Someone out there knew something, but who?

At the station, Kyle bent over a desk, filling out his paperwork, but he couldn't concentrate. Jane's scare a few evenings ago sat on him with the weight of a sumo wrestler. He pressed his fingers against his temples and wished he could push Jane's predicament from his mind so he could finish the work and go home.

He'd only settled one of her problems. He arranged to have the house locks changed...and insisted she leave no key outside. He'd hear about it, for sure, if she locked herself out, but he could live with that. What he couldn't live with was someone harming her.

Jane disturbed his thoughts like a sliver. He couldn't rid himself of the constant worry. He flipped over the report form and doodled on the back.

Kyle searched his mind, seizing every fact he could recall. He dismissed the vandalism situation. That was kids. But he jotted the other incidents on the paper: flat tires, library, cider mill, cat. All those notes but not one fingerprint.

Then he pried names from his mind. Celia, Len, Malik, Keys. Anyone else? The principal came to mind. Skylar? It seemed far-fetched, but Kyle shrugged and added his name to the list. Somewhere in his mind, other phantom characters jogged through his memory, but he couldn't put a name to the faceless people.

"What's up?"

Kyle lurched as a hand slapped his shoulder. "Whoa, George! I'm as bad as Jane."

The other officer straddled a chair beside him.

"I can't get her off my mind," Kyle said.

George let out a loud guffaw. "Situation or woman?"

For a moment Kyle didn't understand. When he did, a surge of awareness shot to his toes. He glanced at George without commenting. "I'm playing detective."

"Why worry now? It's on the books as a break-in."

"Right. Break-in with a key."

George snorted. "Right, those reports go in the circular file." He poked the trash can with his toe.

"So I'm here, playing detective." He pointed to the scribbled notations. "List of suspicious events. List of possible suspects. That's all I have, and I'm sure I've left out suspects."

George leaned over the desk, scanning his chicken scratches. "What about opportunity? Motive?"

Kyle gave a knowing harumph. "Thanks, George. Just get technical."

"Listen, pal, you can't have a crime without a motive." He slid into a chair next to Kyle. "Once you get the list of suspects, check out possible motives and opportunities. At least you can shorten your list."

"Like Celia. I can cross her off right now. She was at the open house with Jane. Plus I was talking to her when Jane was pushed at the cider mill."

"Okay, your list is shorter already."

"I'm forgetting a couple of people she's mentioned, I'm sure." He leaned back in his chair. "The night I met her, she ran into an old high school friend…Perry. I think that's his name. I wonder."

George eyed him. "Suspect list?"

"That…or his memory."

"Memory?" George's mouth pulled to one side.

"Maybe this Perry can recall something. I really think she needs to comb through her past. Redmond is where she grew up. Maybe someone's harboring a grudge."

He knew Jane had said no a million times, but that's where his thoughts kept heading. He leaned back in the chair and swiveled toward George. "She says she can't think of a thing, but maybe Perry can…or his wife. She and Jane were good friends."

George shrugged and mumbled a "maybe."

"I need to hash this over." Kyle snatched up the paper from the desk, folded it and tucked it into his uniform pocket.

Chapter Eleven

Heading toward Perry and Betsy Jones's home, Kyle's shoulder weighted with guilt. His guilt really stemmed from manipulating their visit to her old school friends. When he told Jane he'd like to meet them, he wasn't lying…exactly. But information was his ulterior motive.

Though he'd sifted through every detail, he'd found nothing. And Jane was no help. She continued to dismiss his questions with "I can't think of anything." But learning more about her past riddled his mind with questions, and he couldn't give up.

"Okay," he said, knowing she'd be irritated with him. "Let's go over it again."

She heaved a dramatic sigh. "Kyle, do we have to?"

He ignored her question. "Besides scaring you to death, can you think of any common detail about the incidents? Anything at all, other than the notes?"

"Look, I've been praying so hard to give my fears to the Lord. Now you're riling them up again."

He saw the tension in her face, but he had to stay

hard-nosed. "I know, but I'm a cop, Jane. I'm praying that God protects you, but God made policemen to catch criminals, and since the department isn't actively investigating this, I have to...for your sake. So answer me. Is the note the only similarity?"

Her pained expression tugged at his conscience. He started to withdraw his question, but to his amazement, she answered it.

"Yes," she said, her voice barely audible. For a moment, she paused, then answered his question. "Except for the tires, the note is the only constant. Well, I was alone each time, except for the break-in. Then I wasn't home. But I would have discovered it alone if I hadn't called you."

"Okay." He juggled her data. "You've mentioned the school custodian. And that sub, Dale Keys, who makes you feel guilty for replacing him—and his friend...the art teacher. His name is Larry Fox, right?"

"Yes. But I don't really know him. He's a special in the building. You know, he comes into the school a day or two a week to work with students. Other days he's in different buildings."

"But he'd hear the scuttlebutt, right? He'd know about meetings, open houses, things like that?"

"Sure, but—"

"No buts. If he knows things, he might be involved. Or he could be feeding someone else information. Was he at the open house?"

Jane bit the edge of her lip. "I don't think so, but I could be wrong. Usually the specials don't come to conferences because they work at so many schools."

His jaw felt tight, and he opened his mouth to relax the tension. "Okay. We know Celia was at the open house."

"And at the cider mill. She's a friend, Kyle."

"I'm sorry. I'm just brainstorming."

"Well, 'storm' in some other direction, okay?"

When he looked at her face, Kyle stopped. He was getting nowhere. "Okay, sorry."

She gave him an edgy look.

"Skylar was at the open house, I suppose." He knew she wouldn't mind talking about him. He'd done nothing but knock the stool out from under her since she arrived.

She stared out the passenger window for a moment, then shifted toward him. "He made an opening welcome at six-thirty and a closing speech at nine. That's it. I don't know what he did in between those times."

"That would make a great alibi." He sidled a look at Jane, but she seemed to ignore his comment. "Let's consider possible motives."

She faced him with an arched eyebrow, but didn't say no.

"Skylar?" he asked.

"Doesn't seem to like me. Thinks I'm off-the-wall."

"Not worth tormenting you, I wouldn't think," Kyle said. "He irritates you enough every day."

A hint of a grin shifted across her face.

"Celia... We'll forget her," he said quickly. "Len?"

"I have no idea. Maybe he hates Celia and is really in love with me. He hopes that I'll turn to him in despair and—"

"Nice romance novel, Jane. But let's stick with reality. No reason that you know?"

"I didn't know him when this mess started."

"Okay, but that doesn't mean much. We're speculating. The perpetrator could turn out to be someone you've never met. Then there's that Dale Keys guy.''

"Wants his job back maybe.''

"We don't know that for sure. But at this point, everyone's a possibility. How about that parent...Malik? Far-fetched?''

She glared and hit him with rapid-fire comments. "Far-fetched? How can you say that? He hates me. He hates women. He's the most logical. And he was at the cider mill. Remember that? And...not at the parent conference.'' Her pitch rose with each sentence.

"Yeah, but...I think he's after money. A lawsuit would give him a financial settlement of some kind. Didn't he mention seeing you in court? If he really wanted to hurt you, he'd say nothing.''

She dragged her fingers through her burnished curls. "I suppose you're right.''

She said it, but her disbelieving tone sent another message. "What about the janitor? Any motive?''

"No, he's harmless,'' Jane said. "He's a little slow and watches me a lot. Thinks I'm pretty.''

Kyle struggled to ward off a grin.

"Why are you smiling?'' she asked.

"If I worked there, I'd probably ogle you, too. You're more than pretty. You're beautiful, gorgeous—''

Jane poked him with her elbow. "Get real.''

"I am.'' He could tell she'd had enough. He waylaid his grilling by snapping on the radio. A love song drifted through the speakers. He liked the tune and prayed it would ease the tension he'd aroused with all his prodding.

Soon, Jane pointed to the Joneses' house, and he pulled to the curb in front of the tidy bungalow. Perry opened the door to greet them, and Betsy stood behind him with a generous smile.

After the introductions, Perry invited them into the living room. They settled on the sofa while he plopped into the recliner, and Betsy went to the kitchen for snacks and drinks.

As the evening progressed, Kyle felt antsy, wanting to initiate his questions. He listened patiently while they reminisced about their school days. He hated to ruin their fun, but he hadn't heard a thing that was helpful. Maybe Jane was right. Maybe she'd been that lovable.

When a lull came late in the evening, Kyle jumped in. "So, has Jane told you about her stalker?"

Betsy's large eyes flew open wider. "Stalker? You're kidding." She jerked her head toward Jane. "You haven't mentioned a word."

"I hadn't planned to, either," Jane mumbled.

Her poison-dart look hit Kyle. Bull's-eye. He squirmed. He'd made her angry, but he felt justified.

The term *stalker* captured Perry's attention. "You mean someone's following Jane?"

"And tormenting her. Frightening her to death."

"Who? Why?" Betsy whispered.

"That's what I'd like to find out." Knowing he'd already roused Jane's ire, Kyle told them the story. "I've been asking her about the past. A rival, an enemy, a rejected boyfriend. Maybe a jealous classmate."

They both stared at him with sagging mouths and blank faces. They glanced at each other, then at Jane, but no one opened his mouth.

"So?" Stunned by their silence, he waited. "Any ideas?"

Nothing.

Irritated, Kyle prompted them. "No one? Jane didn't have an enemy in the world? Everyone loved her?"

Their lips curved in unison to an embarrassed grin.

"Right," Betsy said.

Perry leaned forward, resting his elbows on his knees. "This is hard to believe. Jane was like the 'girl next door.' She was always helpful, thoughtful.... Really, I can't think of one negative attribute."

"I can't think of a soul," Betsy agreed.

Like slow motion, Jane turned her head toward Kyle. "I told you."

Kyle released a blast of air. "You did, but I couldn't believe it. You're too perfect."

"She is," Betsy agreed. "Show him one of your diaries, Jane. We used to read them to each other and laugh. Mine was always filled with hateful digs and awful envy. Jane's sounded like the Bible."

Though Kyle heard Betsy's voice, her words faded and his thoughts clung to one word—*diaries.*

Betsy laughed. "I'll never forget one day when—"

Her voice droned on until Kyle gathered his thoughts and unmindfully cut her off. "Jane, you have diaries?"

"I did years ago. Why?"

"You've never mentioned them." He gaped at her surprised face in amazement.

"Why would I? I haven't kept a diary since my freshman year in college." She shook her head. "No, Kyle, I'm sure they'll tell you nothing."

He leaned forward, a hint of promise rising up his spine. "But it's a hope. Maybe some little comment will trigger something. I'm grasping at straws, Jane." He heard his pitch rise but he didn't care anymore. "You want to find out who this jerk is, don't you?"

"Well, yes, but—"

"Then find your diaries and start reading them. It might be an unlikely source, but it's a possibility."

"I have no idea where they are. In the attic? Basement? Maybe thrown away? But I'll look."

"That's all I ask."

"No, you're asking more than that, Kyle. You're asking me to go on a wild-goose chase."

Perry snickered. "I've been on a few wild-goose chases, remember, Betsy?"

Betsy grabbed a pillow from behind her and pitched it at him. "Hush." A bright flush colored her cheeks.

"Silly, maybe, but fun," Perry murmured.

Kyle took advantage of their playful tone. "Come on, Jane. We can have a wild-goose chase of our own. What do you say?"

"Theirs sounds like lots more fun." Finally, Jane gave Kyle a faint grin.

"Hey," Kyle asked her, "ever made out in an attic?"

"No, and I'm not starting now." Her grin deepened to a coy smile. "Look, I'm trying to be angry, and you won't let me."

Kyle nuzzled his cheek against her hair. "The greatest part of being angry is making up."

"See! I can't win. He's always—"

"On a wild-goose chase," Kyle murmured.

On the last Friday in October, Jane and Celia stood outside the school bus door while two other teachers herded the children toward the Pinckney Pumpkin Farm entrance. To Jane's delight, four classes elected to visit the farm for their autumn celebration.

When they'd gathered outside the lodge, scarecrow-costumed employees led the children to wagons. The children giggled at the workers lumbering past with straw sticking from pant legs and sleeves and burlap bags with eye holes covering their heads.

Looking behind her for dawdlers, Jane felt an eerie sensation prickle up her arms. Leaning against the lodge, a scarecrow seemed to follow her movements, but the bag over his head camouflaged his visual direction. He could have been looking at anything. Admitting her recent jitters, she pushed aside her fears.

A scarecrow stepped into line, and Jane jumped, then cringed at her foolishness, realizing the worker was helping the teachers herd the children toward the wagons.

While the children clambered aboard, Jane focused again on the lone scarecrow. He hadn't moved. Could he be a prop? A real scarecrow? She drew in a wavering breath, trying to rid herself of the horrible feeling.

When everyone was accounted for, the horses strained forward and tugged the rigs along the rutted lane past vast furrowed fields. Jane hung on, jiggling and laughing with the children. The bumpy ride was far more pleasant than the fears that rode roughshod through her.

A costumed employee sat with the driver and spoke into a static-filled microphone, describing the process of farming. The students' excitement built as the wagon rumbled into the immense pumpkin field and halted while each child climbed down and selected a pumpkin to paint.

Jane wandered up and down the rows checking on her class and pushed her agitation aside. She had enough to do keeping track of her students, especially Danny Jamieson. With his large brown eyes and spiraling curly hair, he looked as innocent as a lamb…but one in sheep's clothing. She grinned at her analogy.

Jane turned in a slow circle, scanning the broad field and giving a thumbs-up to Celia. Despite her attempt to put her worry aside, Jane glanced around, relieved that the lone scarecrow was nowhere in sight.

Lena and Sara headed toward the wagon, each one carrying a pumpkin. As the others returned, workers helped the children and pumpkins onto the straw-covered floor. When the field emptied, Jane and the other teachers worked their way back to the wagon and their return to the lodge.

At the lodge, children scattered, and Jane scoured the group, counting aloud as she tallied off her students. As she feared, Danny seemed to have vanished.

Moving into the lodge, Jane watched farmhands coach the pumpkin painting, but she stood her vigil, waiting for Danny to appear from the rest room. While she waited, a second grader caught her sleeve.

"Miss Conroy, a scarecrow man said to tell you one of the kids is in the barn."

"The barn?" She gaped at the child, feeling the blood drain from her face. "Are you sure?"

"Uh-huh." The child's head bobbed like an apple in a tub of water.

"Thanks," she said, sensing the child's wide eyes were a reflection of her own. How had Danny roved that far?

Heading for the door, she caught Celia's arm. "Listen, I think Danny wandered off to the barn or something. One of the employees sent a message."

Celia frowned. "Why didn't they bring him back?"

Dismayed that she hadn't questioned that herself, Jane's heart fell to her toes with a new fear. "Maybe he's hurt, and they didn't want…'' Her concern shifted to panic.

''I'll come with you,'' Celia said, falling into step beside her.

''No,'' Jane said, and nudged Celia back toward the others. ''Stay with the kids. I'll be fine.''

Jane raced from the lodge, praying nothing was seriously wrong. Her heart pounded as she rushed toward the barn, fearing the worst.

The door stood ajar.

Adrenaline fired her action. She took a deep breath, tugged back the door and stepped into the dim interior.

When her feet hit the straw-covered floor, terror charged through her. She faltered, peering into the shadows. No one was there. Nothing.

Yet, from inside, she heard a childlike whimper. ''Danny? Danny, are you in here?''

Her voice faded into the dark corners.

Overhead, she heard another sound.

She peered upward toward the dark loft. ''Danny?'' Jane held her breath.

From above, another muffled whimper reached her ears. Her chest tightened against her thundering heartbeat.

''Danny!''

Terror tore through her. She stumbled backward.

No. Not here.

Engulfed by panic, she tried to run from the gloom, but her legs, as if nailed to the floor, held her immobile. Her throat constricted, paralyzing her scream.

Out of the blackness, a body hurled through the air and swung from the rafters.

Her legs buckled, and Jane faded into the darkness.

Chapter Twelve

When Jane opened her eyes, she swallowed a scream. A scarecrow leaned above her, peering into her face. Pale and frightened, Celia gaped at her from the small circle of onlookers. And above her, hanging from the rafters, someone bounced from the end of a rope wearing a dress.

"What...?" She tried to raise her head, but the worker pushed her back. "What happened?"

Celia knelt beside her. "You fainted, Jane, but you're okay."

"Fainted?" Bewildered, Jane focused on the body now being hoisted back up to the loft, a faint memory returning. "Who—?"

"A bad joke," the scarecrow said, patting her arm. "I'm afraid someone hung a real scarecrow from the beam."

Confusion overwhelmed her, and Jane fought to make sense of it. She struggled to remember where she was. "Celia, the children? Danny? Are they okay?"

"They're fine. Danny's with the others. He was

playing around in the men's room.'' She squeezed Jane's arm. ''He's fine.''

Looking up at her friend, Jane sorted the event. ''Who found me?''

''A workman came in and said a woman had passed out in the barn. I came running.''

A feverish breath tore at Jane's chest. Anger, frustration and fear coursed through her. Pressing her elbows against the straw, she tried to lift herself, but hands pushed her back. ''Let me up. Please. I'm okay.''

''Don't let her move yet.''

Kyle's agitated voice sailed through the crowd.

Her head ached and she tried to focus, wondering if he were a wonderful dream. But the scent of his aftershave reached her, validating his presence.

Kyle knelt beside her and slid an arm beneath her, edging her upward. ''Are you sure you're okay? They've called the EMS.''

EMS? No. ''I'm fine, really...but what are you doing here?''

He didn't answer and kept her locked in his grip.

''Kyle, really. I'm fine.''

His look frightened her. He was her safety net and today she saw fear in his eyes.

Releasing his hold, Kyle helped her stand, bolstering her with his arm braced beneath her shoulders.

Her legs were putty, but her determination won the battle. She stood unaided, breathing deeply and trying to sort out what had happened.

''Why are you here?'' she asked again.

''Later,'' he said. ''Tell me what happened.''

She related the story, fighting a tremor that rose from her knees and coursed through her without control.

Celia hovered beside her. "Jane, why do these things keep…"

With a frown, Jane silenced her. Celia eyed the crowd, seeming to understand, and only shook her head.

Kyle guided her outside as an EMS van pulled down the road and stopped. Seeing the vehicle, Jane dug her heels into the ground, but Kyle pushed her forward.

"No," Jane said. "Absolutely not."

Kyle shushed her.

Jane gestured toward the lodge, grateful that the children were still inside painting pumpkins and unaware of the situation. "I have a whole group of kids here, Kyle, and I don't want to scare them. Look I'm standing. Walking." She took a few shaky steps to prove her point.

Nailed to her side, an EMS technician insisted she go to the hospital, prodded by the farm staff who feared a lawsuit, she could only guess. Finally, to get them off her back, she agreed to let them check her blood pressure and pulse.

She sat in the back of the van while they checked her vital signs, and after a lengthy discussion, Kyle convinced them all to release her to his care. The farm staff shuffled off, and the EMS technician climbed into the cab. The van pulled back down the road.

Breathing a relieved sigh, Jane spotted the school group exiting the lodge, toting their decorated pumpkins and gnawing on candy apples.

Celia checked her wristwatch and eyed the group. "Jane, you ride back with Kyle. We have enough adults to handle the kids. Anyway, you're so pale, you'll scare them to death."

Jane hesitated, but knew it was true. The scare had left her shaky and weak.

Celia took a step toward the bus, then paused. "This is another one of those pranks, isn't it?" Celia whispered.

"Pranks?" Her shoulders rose, reliving the horrifying experience. "It's no prank, Celia. The dummy was wearing my dress."

She saw Kyle stiffen. "*Your* dress? Are you sure?" Celia's face contorted with disbelief.

"I think it's one of mine." The image clung in her mind. She could see the line of the dress, the buttons. It was hers, she had no doubt.

Celia gasped. "But how in the world—"

Kyle stopped her in midsentence. "The break-in."

Jane closed her eyes and nodded. "I haven't noticed it missing. But the dress is exactly like mine. It's mine. I know it."

Celia faltered again. "I'd better get going," she said, giving Jane a hug and racing to the waiting bus.

Tears pooled in Jane's eyes, and she reached into her pocket and pulled out a packet of tissues. As she did, a torn slip of paper fell to the ground.

Kyle noticed and retrieved it, then handed it to Jane.

But she froze, repulsed by the paper. It hadn't been in her pocket before. She knew it. She pushed Kyle's hand away from her. "I can't read it. I can't."

Startled, he stared at the dreadful object. "Jane, I thought it was…" He didn't move.

"Read it," she breathed.

He unfolded the paper, then glanced at the words, his face blanching. "It could have been your dress."

"What does it say?"

He held the note up for her to read.

The printed words leaped from the page. *See the rope. See Jane hang.*

Her body swayed, and Kyle gripped her arm, bracing her at his side.

When they were alone, Jane hung her head. "Please, Lord, help me," she whispered. Questions tumbled through her mind. What? Why? Who? She thought of the lone scarecrow and relived over and over the terrifying moment the body hurled from the loft. Whoever was following her had been with her inside the barn, watching.

As they drove, Jane inquired again. "Why were you there…at the farm? I don't understand."

"I heard the dispatch on radio," Kyle said. "Something told me to check it out. I had a bad feeling."

A bad feeling. Jane chastised herself for not using her common sense. Why had she run from the lodge without thinking? But she had. Danny's safety was all she'd considered. An insurmountable weakness washed over her. She let her head drop against the seat and she slept.

When they arrived home, Jane rallied and, without hesitation, checked every closet in the house. Her dress was missing. She had no doubt the one on the dummy was hers.

Kyle insisted she go over the story with him, and she repeated the events, her palm stroking Wilcox's fur as he nuzzled between them on the sofa.

"The story doesn't change, Kyle," she said, losing patience. "I tell it the same way every time."

"What about the whimper you heard?" Kyle probed.

"It had to be the madman imitating a child." She

glared at him. "Is this how you interrogate suspects at the station?"

"No. We use one of those big lights and have a faucet dripping in the background. Drip. Drip. Drip. Finally out of desperation, the culprit confesses."

"Well, you won't get a confession out of me. It's just like I told you."

He slid his arm behind her and drew her closer to his shoulder. She rested her head, and he brushed his fingers along her cheek in a soothing caress. She tried to calm her irritation. It wasn't Kyle, but the situation.

"I'm as frustrated as you, Jane. Nothing makes much sense. I know you think I'm silly, but I really want you to look for those old diaries. Just maybe, something will trigger an idea."

"I haven't had a chance. I'll look as soon as I can." She monitored the frustration etching her voice. The talk seemed ridiculous. Useless.

"How about tomorrow night? We could have a search party," Kyle said.

"I'll look in the daylight." He was pushing again. "It's so gloomy in the attic...and the basement. I'll take care of it tomorrow." She said anything to appease him.

Kyle lay his fingers beneath her chin and tilted her face upward. "I'm telling you, Jane, I'll never forgive myself if anything happens to you. If you get hurt in any way, I don't know what I'll do."

His hand dropped from her chin and he fell against the sofa cushion. "I can't get any more action out of the department. The only real crime is the burglary, and even then the door was opened with a key."

"I know," she said, looking at his face and understanding his frustration. She felt the same. "You've done all you can."

The fire in his eyes softened, and a rush of tenderness eased through her limbs. She'd been tense since the afternoon, but in Kyle's arms she relaxed, feeling safe…and cherished.

Seeing the yearning in his eyes she met his lips in a warm, lingering kiss. She shifted to catch her breath, but Kyle lowered his mouth again, nibbling her lower lip, then kissing her until a sigh trembled from them both.

She drew back, gazing at him with flushed exhilaration. "No bright light or faucet handy, so this is your new technique for a confession," she said.

Kyle laughed. "You like it?"

"Love it," she said. "Better than a glaring bulb or a drip any day."

"I'm glad," he said, drawing her close to his chest. "You'd better get used to it."

Jane reveled in the two weeks that followed. A precious lull enveloped her. The stalker seemed to have vanished. She prayed he was gone for good. Time had flown since she'd first met Kyle. In three days she would celebrate Thanksgiving with his family. Then Christmas was soon to follow.

Though the northern wind had grown colder and promises of snow crept into the weather forecasts, today autumn pirouetted outside her living room window—the last of the burnished leaves dancing on the gusty winds.

Jane's thoughts of Kyle were as bright as the golden landscape, but like the dying leaves, old fears crackled in her thoughts. Could her warm feelings last or would the icy fears of her past kill the love that she felt at this moment?

Guilt filled her. She'd done everything to avoid searching the attic. But hearing Kyle's plea in her ears, Jane pushed her thoughts aside and began her search for the long-forgotten diaries—though she knew they would provide nothing pertinent.

With daylight seeping through the small, dusty windows, she plowed through the attic and located four old leather-bound journals tucked inside a box of her teenage memorabilia. Two books were locked, and she had no idea where the keys were. But she carried them all downstairs anyway.

Expecting Kyle later, she sank into a chair and opened a diary from her sophomore year in high school. The entries sounded foolish. "Got up. Went to school. Did homework. Practiced the piano. Went to Shirley's."

She'd almost forgotten about the piano lessons. Scanning the next few pages, Jane knew she'd been right. Kyle could read her daily accounts until he turned purple, and he'd never find anything helpful.

When she heard the doorbell, Jane dropped the diary, unlocked the door and let Kyle in the house. When he strolled into the living room, a smile lit his face, seeing the four worn, miniature volumes.

He slid his arm around her and kissed her cheek. "You did find them. Thanks."

"I found these four, but two are locked. I suppose I can pry them open. Shouldn't take much."

She handed him one, and he tested the strap's strength by pulling on the closure.

"I'll look for the keys," she said. "They're probably

in the bottom of the box where I found these old things. I can't believe I actually locked them.''

Grinning, he turned the journal over in his hand. ''They held all your secrets.''

She chuckled. ''Right. Read a couple of entries. They'll bore you to tears. 'Got up. Went to school. Went to bed.' That's mighty confidential material, wouldn't you say?''

''That's it? You didn't spill your guts on these pages?''

''I'm not kidding.'' She crossed her heart with her index finger. ''I wasn't sure I wanted you to read about my girlhood antics. But skimming a few entries, there's not one antic that I can see.''

Though he looked disappointed, he winked at her. ''No sense in reading them if I can't get the 'goods' on you.'' He kissed the top of her head.

''Enough silliness,'' she said, giving him a playful shove. ''I have pasta in the oven and a salad in the fridge. Hungry?''

''Sure am,'' he said, shifting his hands to rest on each of her shoulders and, like a caboose, followed her into the kitchen.

After dinner when they'd settled again in the living room, Jane tossed him a diary. ''Have fun.''

He opened the book and delved into the yellowed pages. Before long, Jane laughed and was also reading her mundane, meaningless entries. ''This is ridiculous.''

''You're right,'' Kyle said, closing the book. ''This is getting us nowhere.'' He rose and ambled to the sofa where Jane sat curled in a corner.

She eyed him, guessing what he was up to, but kept her eyes focused on the diary.

Kyle ran his fingers along her arm, then slid his hand behind her neck, distracting her. When she'd had enough, she closed the volume and scowled at him. "Okay, buddy, you were the one who insisted we read these silly things. What's gotten into you?"

"Want the truth?"

"Sure." She held the book in her lap and folded her hands over it like an attentive schoolgirl.

"I can't stop looking at you."

She couldn't stop looking at him, either, but she refused to admit it. "You're supposed to be looking at the diaries."

"But they're boring."

She chuckled. "You can say that again."

"But you're not," he said, his gaze caressing her face. "I think we need to take a break."

With his comment, her earlier hope surfaced, and her humor vanished. "Do you think it's over, Kyle?"

His expression fell. "Over?"

"Over. The stalker. Whatever he is."

A flash of embarrassment flickered on his face.

Jane understood. "You thought I meant *us*."

He averted his eyes. "For a minute."

"That's not what I meant at all." She reviewed the flood of emotions that had washed over his face, then pressed her hand against his with understanding.

She'd struggled with her own wavering feelings— afraid to love him and more afraid if she didn't. Her life had molded around his in these past months. Molded like two complimentary shades of wax forming one lovely candle. But Jane feared her fiery memories. What would happen if her past lit the candle and destroyed the rich, wonderful shape it had taken?

With a curious look, Kyle studied her, but didn't ask

what she meant. Instead, he slid his arm around her back and drew her head to his shoulder. "To be honest, your question threw me. I couldn't imagine that our relationship was over." His gaze captured hers. "You know I love you, Jane."

I love you. His words had struck her ear with so little fanfare, she thought she'd not heard him correctly. "You what?"

"I've fallen in love with you. And don't argue with me. I know how I feel."

The meaning of his words reached her senses slowly. As his message settled in, her pulse soared. She hadn't expected him to say the words aloud. She'd sensed his rising emotions in the past months as she'd felt her own feelings move from friendship to something deeper. But saying the words caught in her throat.

"Just say you feel the same," Kyle said.

Instead of joy, she felt sorrow. Though Jane loved him, she didn't want to. Not yet. Not until she'd dealt with her old hurts and fears. How could she explain it to him?

Kyle clutched her hand. "You're not answering me. I know you feel the same."

She raised her other hand and pressed her palm against his cheeks. "Kyle, I can't deny my feelings. But I have too much to deal with right now. Too many awful memories. Too little time to resolve them."

His expression rent her heart, and she dropped her hand in her lap. "I can't make a commitment until I'm confident that I've resolved the things that have haunted me for so many years. I tried to explain it before."

"I heard you. But I'd hoped." Staring at her pinched

expression, Kyle's stomach churned. The weight of her comment pressed against his own happiness.

"But you didn't believe me," she said.

"I thought when you loved me you'd feel differently."

"I do feel differently, but…if I said that your career doesn't matter, I'd be lying."

"Don't, Jane. Never lie to me."

"I haven't." She closed her eyes. "I'm confused. I'm concerned. I'm cautious. All I can concentrate on right now, Kyle, is what's been happening. When—if—this horrible stalker thing is resolved, I'll have time to work on *me*. It's me, Kyle. I'm the problem. Not you."

She sighed and Kyle held her closer, praying that the words in his head reached her heart. She meant the world to him, and God willing, he'd get her through this horror. No matter what.

The day before the holiday, Jane glanced out the classroom window and watched the snow drifting from the sky. The weatherman had been correct. The city would have a white Thanksgiving.

The flakes had begun the evening before, lightly at first, but by morning, the drive had been long and horrible as she crept along the road to avoid skidding on the slippery streets.

Before classes began, Celia bounded into Jane's room, looking pleased with herself. Len had offered to drive her to school and had even carried in her books. The romantic picture sent a twinge of regret against Jane's heart. Kyle hadn't phoned to offer her a ride. The weight of their discussion lingered in her thoughts.

With the children occupied at their desks, Jane

stripped her bulletin boards of pumpkins, turkeys and Pilgrims and prepared them for the snowflakes and Christmas decorations stored in her closet.

Usually, her students, looking forward to the four-day break, were noisy and hard to control, but today they worked quietly, their noses buried in the math workbooks.

Jane tucked away the last Pilgrim into her closet and ambled through the aisles, checking the students' progress—and her wristwatch—eager for lunch.

As her gaze settled on Lena, she wondered about Sam Malik. He'd seemed to ease off his attack since his last surprise visit. That day he'd left her curious. His only question was whether or not Lena was seeing the special education teacher. Jane had arranged an occasional session—nothing formal—between Lena and Betty Durham from special education. So she was able to answer Malik with a yes. She was thankful, but hoped she wasn't experiencing the proverbial "calm before the storm."

When the lunch bell rang, she shooed the students from the room, locked the door and headed for the teacher's lounge. Stepping inside, her body propelled backward. Standing just within the doorway, Dale Keys eyed her with a grin.

Nodding, she slid into a chair beside Celia. But before she could count to five, Dale had plopped into the vacant spot next to her.

"Surprised to see me?" he asked. "I'm subbing. Fourth grade."

Jane groped for a pleasant expression. "Some of your old students, I suppose," she said, hoping she sounded sincere.

"I prefer third grade, but then, you have my class."

Her shoulders tensed. It was *her* class, but why squabble?

But Celia didn't keep quiet. "That was last year, Dale. This year it's Jane's class."

"Right," he said.

"You're making me feel guilty," Jane said.

Dale chuckled. "Didn't mean to do that. If I hadn't resigned, hoping for something better, I'd still be here."

Curiosity got the better of Jane. "What do you mean 'something better'?"

In a heartbeat, Dale spit it out. "A more cooperative principal, for one."

Surprised, Jane inhaled, and a piece of apple caught in her throat. She coughed and dislodged it. "You shouldn't make me laugh when I'm eating," she said.

Dale shrugged. "Sorry, but it's the truth."

"I know," Jane said, happy to hear she wasn't the only one who found him disagreeable.

After lunch, she promised the students a spelling game to end the day. Anything to get through the last couple of hours. When they were all quiet, Jane reviewed the rules.

"Does everyone understand?"

Head nods and shouts of yes filled the room.

"Okay." She glanced at the ledge below the board, noticing it was empty except for an eraser. "Then all we need is chalk."

Jane opened her desk drawer and withdrew the chalk box while the children waited eagerly. She pulled out two sticks and delved in for two more. She recoiled, feeling a sharp, stinging jab.

Withdrawing her hand, she gaped at the blood seeping from her index finger. Hoping the children hadn't noticed, she hid the wound beneath a tissue from her desk. Blood would frighten the children, especially hers.

Wrapping the cut tightly, she forced a smile to her lips and looked inside the cardboard package. A razor blade stuck upward, and a telltale piece of bloodied paper nestled amid the white chalk.

She eased two more chalk sticks from the cardboard along with the paper and dropped the box into the pocket of her blazer.

"Okay, time to begin." She selected the four students and gave them the signal.

As the children were absorbed with their teams, Jane unfolded the slip of soiled paper, preparing for the worst. Her body quaked as she focused on the note.

Look! Look! Look! See Jane bleed.

Chapter Thirteen

Facing the classroom, Jane leaned her shoulder against the doorframe for support, praying that someone would come by. The blood seeped through the tissue. She needed to clean the cut and find a bandage.

"Jane."

Like an answer to her prayer, she spun around to face Mary Campbell. "Mr. Skylar wants—" She halted. "What's wrong? You look as if you've seen a ghost."

Without details, Jane explained her cut finger.

"Bandages are in the workroom cabinet," Mary said. "Go ahead, and I'll stay here a couple of minutes."

Thanking Mary, Jane hurried toward the office. At this point, she didn't care what Skylar wanted. She wanted a bandage and to know how the razor blade got into her chalk box.

Rounding the corner, Jane spied Charlie ducking into a custodian's closet, his rolling trash container lagging a little behind him.

"Charlie," Jane called out, remembering he had a key to her room.

He peeked around the door, his mouth gaping.

"Did you let anyone into my classroom this morning?"

He drew back, shaking his head. "N-no. Rules say I c-can't. Just y-you or a sub."

She showed him her bloodied tissue-wrapped finger.

He gaped at it, then scowled.

"Someone slipped a razor blade in the chalk, and I cut myself," Jane said in explanation.

"A r-razor?"

His startled expression looked sincere. "It's okay, Charlie. I'm fine." Still, she wondered. He had a key to her room, and weeks earlier, she'd stumbled on him putting the chalk box into her desk. Could it be?

As Jane entered Redmond Community Church for the Thanksgiving Day worship service, Kyle guided her into a front pew, his dark gray suit accentuating his tall, powerful frame. Jane struggled to keep herself from admiring him as he helped her pull off her coat.

Once seated, Kyle held her hand, avoiding the one with the bandage. The evening before, she'd reviewed with him the events of her day: Charlie, the razor blade and her horrible run-in with Skylar while searching for a bandage.

After telling Skylar about the razor blade incident, he'd only quizzed her about Lena and the special education teacher Betty Durham. Jane had struggled with her response.

But instead of defending the special help she'd arranged for Lena she poked her throbbing finger in his face. "What about the razor blade? And the note?" she had asked.

"Be more careful next time" was all he'd said.

Drawn from her recollection by the swell of the church organ, Jane sighed and glanced at the tape around her finger, then at Kyle's powerful profile. As always in his presence, Jane felt safe, his broad shoulder pressing against hers and his ample hand wrapped around her smaller one.

Would she ever rid herself of the awful fear that hovered on the fringe of their relationship? She knew it was foolish. Kyle and her father were different men. Different cops.

But could she trust Kyle to stay as gentle as he was now? Would the stress of his career bring him home some evening, frustrated and angry, his voice shaking the rafters, his fists hammering the table?

Or like the rumors about her father, would a crafty criminal tempt Kyle to overlook a crime or destroy evidence? Would she wait for him to come home...and learn that he'd been wounded or, worse, killed?

She pushed the tumbling questions from her mind and drew in Kyle's familiar fragrance, a subtle, woodsy aroma that caused her pulse to surge, just thinking of his nearness—the sweet kisses and tender retreat that left her wanting more.

Shame shuffled through her as she lifted her eyes to the stained glass window. Today was Thanksgiving. Instead of dwelling on her problems, she should give thanks and praise God for keeping her safe...and giving her Kyle.

Her gaze swept the sanctuary, adorned for the occasion with harvest symbols—cornstalks, fruits and vegetables, homemade preserves and giant pumpkins.

Seeing the pumpkins sent a tremor of fear down her spine.

When Kyle's father stepped into the pulpit, Jane had no trouble concentrating. His commanding voice and powerful messages lifted her spirits, and when the service closed with the Doxology, Jane sang with fervor, praising God for all His good gifts.

Kyle's mother joined them as they waited at the exit. Strangely, Jane had begun to feel like one of them. Unwise, she told herself.

On the way to his parents' house, Kyle seemed distracted and withdrawn. Jane studied him, sensing that something weighed on his mind.

"A dollar for your thoughts," she said.

He glanced her way with a faint grin. "Inflation?"

She nodded. "Something's bothering you."

"A bit."

"What is it?"

He rubbed his temple without answering.

Though harnessed by the seat belt, she shifted slightly toward him. "You can tell me. What did I do?"

"Nothing. It's just stress, I think."

"Stress? You're worried about me. I shouldn't have told you about the razor blade."

He glimpsed at her, his face breaking into a pitiful grin. "No, Jane, it's not you. I'm glad you told me. You shouldn't keep anything from me."

"Then something's going on at work?"

"Right, but it's nothing you should worry about."

Jane arched her brow. "You shouldn't keep anything from *me*, either."

He flashed a guilty look. "I'm expecting a small scene with my dad today. The department's been working on a series of armed robberies—two men who hold up small gas stations and party stores. I know Dad reads that stuff in the paper. Today he'll ply me with questions. I can't lie to him.''

She scowled. ''Why would you lie?''

''Not lie, exactly. I've been called to the scene a couple of times, but we're always there after the fact.''

''Guns?'' Jane asked.

His mouth curved to a wry grin. ''Yes, they're armed.''

He ran his hand over her shoulder and caressed her jaw with his fingers. ''Please don't worry.''

Jane bent her head toward his hand, enjoying the sweet sensation. But the unpleasant thought of Kyle being in danger plastered itself in her mind. Her razor blade problem sounded foolish in comparison.

Her stomach tightened as her mind marched backward in time, thinking of the worried hours her mother spent waiting for her father to return home every day. Drugs, gambling, money laundering—all those crimes meant danger. She looked at Kyle's handsome profile. How could she allow herself to fall in love with someone in the same dangerous business? The answer evaded her. But in truth, she had already fallen in love. Now, what could she do about it?

When they arrived at his folks' house, the aroma of turkey and stuffing already filled the air. She joined Ruth in the kitchen while Kyle and Paul talked in the living room and watched a pregame football program on television.

Ruth had everything under control, but Jane finished setting the table, and finally the time came to carry in the food.

When they gathered around, the family joined hands,

Jane clasping Paul's on one side and Kyle's on the other. As each shared his own personal thanksgiving, Jane felt the strength and comfort of the two men beside her. After the blessing, she filled her plate and enjoyed a rare home-cooked holiday meal...with a family.

Later in the living room, Kyle and his father talked sports and stared at the television on one side of the room while Ruth and Jane, to Kyle's obvious dismay, huddled on the sofa, looking through old photograph albums.

Kyle pulled himself from his conversation to toss a point to his mother. "You don't have to give Jane a biography of my life, Mom. You'll scare her off."

Jane swatted at him from across the room. "Pay attention to the football game and let us be." Yet teasing him, she looked again at his adorable photo and cooed, "You were so-o-o cute, Kyle. Look at that spiky brown hair and those mischievous blue eyes."

Kyle eyed the photograph she held up for him. "That haircut wasn't my fault."

"Oh, really?" Paul commented.

Ruth leaned toward her in a whisper. "He found scissors. Did a little trim of his own."

Like a soothing balm, the feeling of family washed over Jane again. Never in her life had she sat around the living room relaxing with her parents. Her dad's work schedule had been unpredictable, and her mother too often seemed withdrawn and unapproachable. With no brothers or sisters, "family" was an unknown entity. But today she luxuriated in the warm, comfortable sensation.

Kyle sidled another look at Jane and his mother. His parents' fondness for Jane was blatant. He'd tried to move slowly—as slowly as he could with his heart on a high-speed chase. He didn't want to scare her off.

He'd watched her struggle with their relationship, but understood. He believed with all his heart that she loved him. If she didn't, his parents' obvious doting could send her packing.

He enjoyed watching his mother and Jane collaborate like two old friends, chuckling together and poring over the old albums. She loved him. She had to.

"Did you hear me, Kyle?" Paul asked.

Kyle's head pivoted from Jane toward his father. "Sorry, Dad, I was thinking."

Amusement rose on Paul's face. "Sure you were."

Kyle steered him away from any more comments. "What were you saying?"

"I talked to Walter Kitzmiller the other day."

"Kitzmiller?"

"Walter from the Rotary Club—you remember him."

"Sure...I guess. So what's up with old Walter?" Kyle grinned, but Paul raised an eyebrow. Seeing his father's sincerity, Kyle struggled to look interested.

"He owns the White Knights Security and Surveillance Services."

"Oh, right." Kyle knew him, and now he'd caught on. The conversation was leading where he didn't want to go, and his gut tightened.

"Sometime after the first of the year, he'll be looking for an administrator," Paul said, dropping the information with as much nonchalance as a hippo on a tightrope. "Someone to run the business for him."

"I see." And Kyle did, but he wouldn't make it easy. His father's expression pulled at his conscience.

He understood too well, but a desk job wasn't what Kyle wanted. Would his dad ever understand?

"You ever think about that, Kyle? Security?"

"No, Dad. Never." Though his eyes were focused on his father, in his peripheral vision, he saw Jane's attention turning to their conversation.

"Good pay. Real good pay," his father said.

"Really? You thought I might be interested?"

Paul shrugged. "Maybe. He told me. I'm telling you."

Kyle swallowed the burning bile stinging his throat. "I don't want to disappoint you, Dad, but that's not my line of work. I can't imagine myself—"

"Just thought I'd mention it," Paul said, obviously struggling to cover his disappointment. "Something to think about."

Kyle nodded his head. "Sure."

But it wasn't something for Kyle to think about. He glanced at Jane and saw her pained expression. She'd overheard, and Kyle wondered what had been said that upset her. When he caught her eye, Jane looked the other way, returning to her own conversation with his mother.

Paul retrieved the folded newspaper next to his chair and placed it on his lap.

The bold headlines of the serial-style holdups glared like a spotlight, and Kyle knew his other worry was becoming a reality.

"I was noticing, there's been a series of holdups in the area." Paul pointed to the paper. Though his question sounded casual, Kyle recognized his dad's concern.

Kyle shot a quick "I told you so" look at Jane. "Yes, it's true."

"Any leads?"

"A couple."

"Guns?"

"Yes."

If the situation weren't filled with tension, Kyle might have chuckled at their controlled conversation, each struggling to keep his voice cool and calm. Neither fooled the other one, nor themselves.

"Kyle said he always gets called after the fact," Jane blurted, apparently uncomfortable with the tension.

Irritation jackknifed through Kyle, but he recovered. He understood that Jane thought it would alleviate his father's fears. But Kyle knew better.

"Oh," his father asked, "you've been on duty then?"

"Yes, Dad. I know you're worried, but don't be. It's part of the job."

At that point, Kyle gave up. While he laid out the details, his father listened with deep concentration etched on his face.

When he'd finished, Kyle leaned back, waiting for his father's retort. But his father's loving response hit Kyle harder.

"I'll keep you and your department in my prayers," Paul said.

Kyle grimaced, sorrowed by the pain he was causing. "Thanks, Dad. I appreciate that."

Paul's grim face flashed a heartrending grin. "Son, you know that you're always in my prayers."

"I know. Now, let's talk about something more... general."

A heavy silence hung on the air. The four sat gaping at one another at a loss for words until their uneasiness turned to laughter and lightened the uncomfortable moment.

When his mother mentioned pumpkin pie, Jane rose to help, but his dad jumped from the chair and volunteered.

Jane sank into the cushion, and Kyle took the opportunity to join her on the sofa.

"I hope you're not bored with all the albums and, well, my dad's comments. I knew this would happen."

Jane shook her head. "I've liked your folks from the day I met them, Kyle. They're wonderful. I'm crazy about them."

"What about their son?"

"He's not bad...most of the time."

Kyle did a double take. "What does that mean?"

Jane leaned against the corner of the sofa, distancing herself from him. "I don't like the tension I felt between you and your dad. There must be a better way to handle that."

"Tell me how, Jane?" His father's words marched through his head. After the first of the year, Walter Kitzmiller would need someone to run his security company. What was he supposed to say? Should he consider a desk job...for his dad? For Jane?

His heart tumbled to his toes and a prayer rose in his thoughts as he considered his parents and Jane. *Lord, what am I to do?* He'd make three people happy if he left the force. *Is that what I should do, Lord? Please give me guidance.* Jane's voice brought him back to the present.

"I can't tell you what to do, Kyle. But I know how they feel."

He heard his parents' voices in the kitchen and, fearing they'd return, he hurried his thoughts. "I love my parents…and you know, I love you with all my heart, Jane. But we're talking about my career. My life. Please tell me you love me.''

What he was expecting, Kyle had no idea. He needed to know for sure. If he had life-changing decisions to make, he needed her assurance.

Jane's eyes filled with tears. ''Yes, Kyle…yes, I love you. But I need time. I have a lot of thinking to do. I can't imagine losing you.''

His belly tightened with her confession, but sadness weighted his chest, seeing the tears in her eyes.

''I've been frightened with all the goings-on, and the thought of facing this awful situation without you is unbearable. I'm praying it's over. Then, maybe, I can think about us.''

''You're worth waiting for,'' he said.

He viewed her strained face and lifted his hand, smoothing away the furrows of stress and sadness. With his index finger, he traced the line of her lips.

A faint smile touched her face, the tension fading. She lifted her hand and pressed the palm against his roving fingers.

''You have great lips, Jane. Meant for my kisses.''

Jane's pulse surged, and she raised her mouth to meet his eager mouth, molding together a perfect fit. His tender touch roused her, tugged out her inner strength and drew her into reality. How could Kyle hurt her? How could he disappoint her? How could he ever deceive her?

She relaxed, her gaze drawn to his full, promising lips and his adoring eyes. Where was her faith in God? Where was her trust in Kyle? He'd proved himself over and over. So had God. But she lived with her fears…the black demons of uncertainty that tore away her judgment and shredded her common sense.

Like a child fearing the monster beneath her bed, Jane had lived with her feet hidden beneath the covers of warped memories, never touching the floor of truth.

She'd accepted the dark without searching for the light. The Lord was her light, and Kyle was God's star, an earthly light to lead her away from the darkness. The meaning rolled through her.

Her prayer rose from the depth of her soul, a prayer for Kyle and for herself.

Chapter Fourteen

Following Thanksgiving, the Christmas spirit hit the shopping centers first, and then Jane. The next two weeks danced by in a flurry of Christmas programs, shopping, decorating and one heavy snowfall. Jane thanked God each morning for the busy, yet uneventful days. Once again it seemed her tormentor had stepped from the face of the earth.

When the spirit hit her, one of the first things she did was hunt in the attic for the nostalgic Christmas ornaments that had belonged to her parents: the hand-carved crèche, the porcelain angels. So many childhood memories. She located them, and with a few nostalgic tears she carried them down the stairs.

Though uncertainty lay in her future with Kyle, Jane refused to let her fears dampen the moment. She looked forward to Christmas with him and his family, and she'd enlisted Kyle to help her select a gift his parents would enjoy.

Dressing in a comfortable pair of skidproof shoes, soft sweater and warm slacks, she waited for him to arrive. The thought of shopping with Kyle wrapped her in a cozy mood.

When the bell sounded, Jane hurried to answer. When she snapped on the porch light, the fanlight over the door remained dark. Apparently the bulb had burned out, and she grinned, knowing Kyle could replace the light without using a step stool. She flung the door open.

No one.

Apprehension slithered up her spine. Through the storm door glass, she scanned the empty porch.

Then she saw the box.

With her heart pounding, Jane clutched the door frame, a roar rising in her ears. Gathering her wits, she slammed the door, leaning against it as fear gripped her. Why? Why when she'd just begun to relax and think it was over?

Headlights flickered across the living room wall. Then footsteps sounded on the porch, and when the bell jangled, although anticipated, Jane flinched.

"Kyle?" she gasped, waiting for a response.

"Jane, open up."

When she recognized his voice, she flung open the door.

A deep frown furrowed his face. "What's wrong?" He held the box in his hand.

Her repressed tears broke loose and streamed down her cheeks.

Kyle grabbed the storm door, wrenching it open. In a heartbeat, he stood at her side, and she clung to his powerful chest, letting her tears flow.

"What happened?" he asked.

"The box," she said between gasps. "I prayed it was over."

His brows knitted. "The box?" He glanced at the small cardboard container in his hand.

"Someone rang the bell, and when I opened the door, no one was there. Only the box."

"But you haven't looked inside," he said. "Maybe a neighbor dropped off some Christmas cookies or..."

"Kyle," Jane said, "my neighbors don't leave packages and run away."

He shrugged and put the carton to his ear. "Well, it's not ticking."

"I know you're trying to make me relax, but it's not working. Please open it. I can't look." She closed her eyes and waited, her heart pounding in her throat.

"Photographs" was all he said.

Her eyes opened. "Photographs?" She faltered, seeing the distress in his face.

"Handle them by the edges," he said, dropping the photos in her palm.

When she saw them, her heart plummeted. "They're all me."

Carefully she shuffled through them, fear rising to a hum in her ears. "Look," she said, indicating the snapshot, "I'm in the school parking lot and coming out of the house." Her voice caught in her throat. "And, Kyle, here we are on Thanksgiving...going into church." Her heart hammered against her chest.

Trancelike, Kyle stared at the photos.

"And here," she moaned, poking at the photograph, "I'm in my classroom. It's through the window. How could someone do this without me seeing him?"

"With a telephoto lens. He could be on the street in his car." Kyle's disheartened voice faded.

Kyle stared at the photos again. "Let me take this

to the station. They'll look for fingerprints. The emulsion makes a great print.''

''Really?''

''And the box. The lab can do wonders.'' Holding the picture by the edges, he dropped them back into the box.

Irritated with himself, Kyle harnessed his anger. He was letting this affect him too much. He wasn't thinking clearly. He looked at Jane's pale face. ''Do you want to forget shopping?'' he asked, seeing the stress in her eyes.

''No, we need to eat…and I have to get over this. Can you wait a few minutes so I can get myself back together?''

Kyle gazed at her tear-streaked face, and he ached. ''Take all the time you need, and while you're getting ready, I'll go out and check around the house.''

When Jane left the room, Kyle pulled the small slip of paper from his pocket, feeling guilty that he'd hid it from her when he saw it inside the box. Anger rose in him like bile. He didn't have to read the note to know the pattern. He unfolded it, and his stomach knotted.

See Jane. See Jane live?

He stared at the question mark, relieved that he'd found the note, instead of Jane. The department had to take the situation seriously now. He fought the tremor that shot to his hand, folded the note and dropped it beneath the photographs, then closed the box lid.

He loved Jane, and now he understood how violence could surface in a usually calm, rational person. He wanted to hurt this sick man for the pain he caused her.

He tucked the box under his arm and stepped outside. Slipping the carton into the back seat of his car,

Kyle grabbed a flashlight and followed the heavy-booted footprints through the shrubs. He crouched and studied the waffle pattern of the sole imprinted in the melting snow. The prints led to the street.

His anger dissipated in the cold air. Instead, he remembered his father's lessons, and he knew what God expected. Though his work dealt with man's law, he was led by God's. Punishment was not his business, but finding the stalker was.

When he returned inside, Jane had reappeared looking lovely again. Only slight tension around her eyes offered a telltale sign of her distress. He described the boot print as they left to drop the evidence off at the police department before going for dinner and Christmas shopping.

The subject of the situation arose again after they returned home.

"Sit in the living room, and I'll put on some coffee." Jane gestured to the recliner chair, but Kyle stepped along with her as she headed to the kitchen.

"I'll stick with you. How's that?" His eyes shifted from side to side scrutinizing every nook and corner. "Before I leave, I'll check outside again. No doubt the guy was long gone before you opened the door, but I'll rest easier if I make certain."

A shiver ran up Jane's arms, and looking at his face, she knew he had his own fears. "Thanks." A heavy sigh escaped her as her mind shuffled through the things that had happened. She glanced at him over her shoulder as she filled the pot with water. "I keep asking myself the same question. What have I done to someone?"

"Well, I'll tell you one thing." He leaned against

the kitchen counter beside her. "Whoever this is wants to be caught."

She spun around. "Wants to be caught? Why?"

"He wants to be stopped. He's taking chances. If you'd answered the door fast enough, you might have recognized him."

"Even if I knew him, it was dark. The porch light's burned out."

Burned out? The man was smart. "And how did he know the light wouldn't come on, Jane?"

She scowled. "I don't know. How?"

"I'm guessing he unscrewed the bulb. I'll check when I leave." He shifted from the counter and sat at the table. "If not, I'll put a new one in for you. How's that?"

"Thanks," she said, lifting the cups from the cabinet, questions spinning in her mind. Why would someone want to get caught? Was the man afraid of what he would ultimately do? Could that be it? Fear gripped her, and she clung to the edge of the counter. *Please, God, help me.*

With her back to Kyle, she slid a few chocolate-chip cookies on a plate, taking time to control herself. She didn't need to upset him any more than he already was.

When she turned around with the treats, Wilcox wrapped around her ankles.

"Old Will wants his dinner, I see," Kyle said, reaching down and capturing the cat's face in his fingers. "Eat your own food, pal. I'm not sharing."

Jane grinned and set the plate on the table, then filled Wilcox's dish. When the coffee was done, she poured the hot brew into two mugs and slid one to Kyle, then sat beside him.

He lay his hand on hers. "I hate to ask, but have

you gone through those two locked diaries? For some reason, I feel the key to this thing is there."

"No. And speaking of keys, I found the two keys for the diaries when I was getting down some Christmas decorations, but what good is 'I washed my hair'? That's about as newsy as the other diaries have been."

Kyle sipped the coffee, then lowered the cup and pushed it by the handle in concentric circles on the table. "How about in your senior year, Jane? Why were two diaries locked? Maybe they'll tell something." He raised his eyes to hers. "Think back."

She shook her head. "Please, not tonight, Kyle. I'll read them, I promise."

He nodded and they sat in silence for a while until the conversation drifted to her staff Christmas party the next evening. Sooner than she wanted, Kyle rose.

"I'd better let you get to bed," he said. "Big party tomorrow."

She nodded, rising from her chair. He slipped his arm around her shoulder, and she walked with him to the door.

Before he stepped outside, Kyle placed a hand on each of her shoulders. "Now, lock the door as soon as I leave. Don't answer it for anyone unless you know for sure who it is. Do you understand?"

"I will," she said.

When he pulled his hands away and opened the door, a sense of impending loneliness riffled through her.

He kissed her cheek gently. "You'll be fine. Please, don't worry."

"Okay," she said, her voice a whisper.

"I'll be by to pick you up around seven tomorrow for your Christmas party, okay?"

"Seven's good."

He grinned. "Nothing can happen at a party."

She gave him a feeble smile.

Outside, he fumbled with the porch light. "It'll work now," he said. Jane nodded and closed the door, then turned the lock. She leaned her back against the jamb. Was Kyle right about nothing happening at the party? She wasn't sure she'd be safe anywhere.

Chapter Fifteen

Students arrived in the morning, excited, and bearing holiday gifts: scarfs, handkerchiefs, bath powder, ornaments and candy. When Lena came through the door, her face glowed as she handed Jane a telltale box. Jane didn't have to open it to know it was chocolates.

"How sweet. Thank you." She patted the girl's thin shoulder. "Tell your mom I said thanks, okay?"

Lena glanced at her with a timid grin. "And my daddy."

A knot twisted in Jane's stomach. "Sure, and your daddy."

Jane glanced at the box, wondering if the gift could possibly have Sam Malik's approval. She placed the package in her locked closet for safekeeping, and the day began.

The staff bustled with excitement, looking forward to the evening's Christmas party. This year, Celia had procured her condo's clubhouse, and to Jane's surprise, the usual dour Skylar agreed to provide all the catered food.

When the school day ended, Jane rushed home and dressed in her green silk pants and tunic. She was determined to have a good time despite the latest problem. For fun, she draped red, green and silver beads around her neck and fastened on a pair of Christmas ornament earrings.

Completing her makeup, Jane reminisced how she and Kyle had become a couple in a wonderful sort of silent understanding. Though the word *love* had been spoken, *marriage* had not, and Jane wondered if it were possible. But instead of worrying, she was learning to enjoy each moment. She'd had enough things to worry about to last a lifetime.

While waiting for Kyle, she opened Lena's box of candy and studied the chocolates. One appeared to be her favorite: mint. She nibbled the edge, frowning when she tasted coconut. She eyed another, and this time she grinned as she bit into a tangy peppermint bonbon.

Outside, an automobile sounded on the driveway, and she put the lid back on the guilt-infested box and slid it out of sight. How could Lena know she absolutely loved chocolate? The rich brown confection was her nemesis.

Kyle came to the door in his dark slacks and bright red sweater. They chuckled, looking like Christmas elves in their red and green garb.

"Piece of candy," she asked, lifting the lid from the box.

He glanced inside, then shook his head. "I'll save myself for the party. You told me it was catered."

"It is," she said, putting the candy aside and slipping on her coat. She grabbed her purse and they were out the door.

Within minutes, they arrived at the clubhouse. The sound of Christmas music wove through the background chatter, and a piano in the corner suggested possible carols later in the evening.

As Jane slipped off her coat in the open foyer, Celia came through the archway. "There's a coatrack through the door there," she said, pointing to Jane's left.

Kyle took their coats, and Jane followed Celia into the large room. Pausing to survey the crowd, she eyed the caterers carrying in trays of cold appetizers and filling chafing dishes with hot hors d'oeuvres. The aroma of meatballs and chicken mingled with cranberry-scented holiday candles.

"Where's Len?" Jane asked, surveying the room.

Celia arched an eyebrow. "Pouting somewhere."

"Pouting?"

She shrugged, and Jane let it drop.

When Kyle stepped to her side, he slipped his arm around Jane's shoulder. "Food smells good, and I skipped dinner." He gave her a wink.

"There's plenty," Celia said. "Look at it all."

Kyle glanced at the holiday table, then scanned the guests. "Len's busy?"

Jane nuzzled his arm. "Pouting."

Kyle eyed her. "Pouting? Are you serious?"

Celia shook her head and took a backward step. "I think this is where I came in. Kyle, hunt him up, will you?"

"Sure," he said as Celia retreated. "Something must be wrong."

Jane shrugged, thinking the same thing. "Why don't you scout around and try to smooth his ruffled feathers?"

Kyle slipped away, and Jane ambled around the room, stopping periodically to chat. Finally Kyle returned with Len who, in spite of Celia's comment, looked cheery.

"The lost is found," Kyle said. "Had his head in a case of champagne."

Len chuckled. "I was putting it on ice." He glanced at their empty hands. "No drinks yet? The bar's set up over there." He gestured toward the far wall where a table was spread with wines and soft drinks.

"Thanks," Jane said. "I might like a soda."

"Same here," Kyle agreed.

A wry smile rose on Len's lips. "Soda?" He shrugged. "Help yourselves."

Kyle steered her to the table, and while he poured the soft drinks, Jane scanned the guests, noticing Larry Fox across the room with Dale Keys at his side. She poked Kyle. "See the two guys by the piano?"

Replacing the bottle cap, Kyle glanced up and nodded, then handed Jane a glass.

She lowered her voice. "The one with the fisherman knit sweater is the art teacher. The other is Dale Keys. I wonder why he's here."

Kyle's cop persona took over, scrutinizing Keys. "Seems normal to me. They both worked with these people, Jane."

"I suppose."

"Retired officers and part-timers drop by the station and show up at parties all the time."

Kyle's stomach rumbled, and he took Jane's arm and followed the hoards who descended on the table like vultures, snatching up the holiday plates and loading them with ham, meatballs and shrimp.

When he and Jane settled on a small sofa, Celia hurried up and squeezed in beside. Len sat on the arm, balancing his plate on his knee. The conversation lulled as they concentrated on the food.

"I'm going back for seconds," Len said, taking a big swig from a plastic champagne glass. "Anyone else?" He surveyed them, then picked up an empty glass. "Jane, how about another soda?"

"Thanks. I could use something cold. Ice, too, please."

"You got it," he said, swaggering away.

Celia glanced at them, her face unsmiling. "Len drinks too much."

Jane nodded. "Tonight's the first time I noticed. Maybe it's just the holiday." She handed Kyle her empty plate, and he set it on the floor.

Celia shrugged. "I'll tell you one thing. He doesn't like to hear about it."

"Men don't like to be told anything, Celia," Kyle said, hoping to offer a bit of humor, but her face remained etched with irritation.

"Is that why he was upset?" Jane asked.

She rolled her eyes. "I had the audacity to ask him to watch how much he drank."

Kyle listened halfheartedly, wondering if Len really had a problem. Watching Len cross the floor, Kyle was distracted by a flash of light, and he turned in that direction. The art teacher focused a camera on a group of posed teachers, adjusting the settings. While Kyle watched him, Len returned.

Larry Fox and his camera traveled from one group to another around the room, snapping people in various party modes. Dale Keys followed, nibbling from a holiday plate.

As the twosome neared, Len rose from the sofa arm.

"Look who's here." He sauntered to Dale's side, and they shook hands.

As they chatted, Kyle kept his eyes focused. The men laughed and slapped each other on the back unaware that Kyle studied them like suspects until the situation seemed ludicrous. None of them looked dangerous.

Keys peered at the pile of sweets on his plate. "I really overdid this. Anyone?" He held the plate out to the group. No one accepted his offer. "If I don't see you again, Jane, have a merry Christmas."

He grabbed a small pecan tart from his plate and dropped it into her hand. "And don't say I never gave you anything." He chuckled, shoving the plate toward the others.

Everyone declined again, and Jane murmured a weak thanks, flashing Kyle a helpless grin and cradling the tart in her hand. Sometimes Dale did seem odd.

Kyle studied the man, wondering what made someone that obnoxious. Jane said it. Keys liked attention.

Finally, Larry focused the camera and had them squeeze together while he snapped their photograph. When the light flashed, Len leaped from the sofa arm, snatched the camera and staggered backward, flailing his arms for the two men to pose with the group. Len focused and refocused. Finally the camera flashed again.

His thoughts flying to the box of photographs on Jane's porch, Kyle studied the men. They both looked comfortable using the lens.

Wishing he could push the surveillance from his mind, he covered a yawn. He had had enough for one night and longed to make a quick getaway. But it was Jane's Christmas party. He pressed his tense back muscles against the sofa and watched Skylar cruise the room, flaunting a pleasant expression on his usual unsmiling face. Kyle swallowed a chuckle, thinking of the Grinch that stole Christmas.

When a crowd formed around the piano, Jane rose and beckoned him to follow her toward the music. Kyle stood behind her. As she leaned her weight against him, he wrapped his arms around her waist and nestled against her. He enjoyed the closeness and loved the sense of wholeness he felt.

Soon, Jane joined the singing while Kyle listened, admiring her full, clear voice. But when she became quiet, Kyle sensed something wrong. He'd noticed her body tense earlier, and when she fidgeted again, he whispered in her ear. "Tired of standing?"

She looked at him over her shoulder. "I'm not feeling well." Perspiration covered her forehead.

"Something didn't agree with you."

She offered a feeble grin. "Or I ate too much. I feel strange. Woozy."

He chuckled remembering her near-empty plate compared to his own piled high with food. "I'll get you some club soda. It might settle your stomach."

She nodded, and Kyle slid through the crowd, heading for the drink table.

When he stepped away, Jane's knees buckled. She braced herself against the edge of the piano. Her stomach had been churning for the past fifteen minutes, but she'd thought the feeling would disappear. Now a deep wave of pain rolled through her. As the pressure bore down, a wave of nausea overwhelmed her until it subsided again.

Kyle returned with the drink, and she sipped it, but the cramp knifed with greater speed, and the cold sweat ran from her forehead. She didn't want to ruin the evening, but the sensation frightened her.

Kyle studied her, and his face echoed the concern in his voice. "Jane, you're sick. We'd better leave."

Weakness overtook her, and she could only nod. Kyle supported her under the elbow, and they moved through the crowd with as much speed as Jane could muster. The acute pain racked through her body, and fear jackknifed in her mind. She wondered if she might lose consciousness.

Kyle grabbed their coats, and as they reached the exit, Kyle motioned to Celia. Following his rapid, but limited explanation, he and Jane stepped outside into the brisk night air.

"I'll get the car," Kyle said while Jane leaned against the building.

"Too much to drink?" a voice asked from the darkness after Kyle had left.

Jane gasped, her stomach rising to her throat. Dale stepped into the dim alcove, a cigarette dangling from his lips.

The smoke made her more nauseated. "No, I'm not feeling well."

"That's too bad." When Kyle rolled to the entrance, Dale tossed the butt and grasped the door handle. "Have a nice holiday," he said.

As Dale sauntered into the building, Kyle hurried to her side. "Who was that?"

"Dale." The sharp knifing pain returned, and she clenched her teeth to control the wave of nausea.

He edged her toward the car, but hesitated. "I think I'm going to be sick."

"Don't worry about it." He bolstered her elbow, easing her into the car.

Before he closed the door, she grabbed his arm. "And, Kyle, please, just take me home." If she could only lie down and rest, she'd be okay. Anything to make the surging cramps go away.

Kyle slid into the driver's seat and pulled out of the parking lot. Jane's head dropped against the seatback, and when he turned toward the hospital, she felt too weak to argue. Jane wrestled with her questions. What was wrong with her? The flu? Food poisoning? She feared she would die, then wished she would as the next throbbing pain rolled through her.

When Kyle reached the hospital, the sign blurred, and a moan escaped her lips. She squeezed her eyes together to keep her tears at bay.

Gripping the steering wheel, Kyle stared ahead and pulled up to the emergency entrance. As he jumped from the car, a security guard had already opened Jane's door and pulled a wheelchair forward. With Jane settled in the chair, Kyle gave her shoulder a squeeze and left her in the guard's hands while he parked.

Kyle stared at his shaking hands. Emergencies were his job, but tonight, fear gripped him despite his experience with crisis. This was Jane, not some stranger. He loved her. That made the difference, and at the moment he fretted. He sorted the possibilities. Appendix? Flu? Food poisoning?

After parking, Kyle darted through the emergency doors and scanned the area. Jane sat in an alcove, wearing a blood pressure cuff. Approaching, he faltered, noting her blood pressure: 180 over 120. Too high. Way too high. Heart rate: 130. Bad.

He listened while the admissions nurse read off the list of questions. As Jane faded into throes of pain,

Kyle responded for her. "We're coming from a Christmas party."

"When did the pain begin?" the nurse asked.

"About a half hour or forty-five minutes ago, I think. I'm not exactly sure. We came directly here."

She jotted the information onto the clipboard form. "She ingested food?"

"Yes, but not much. We ate just about the same foods." Except he'd eaten much more.

Hearing a quiet moan, Kyle's jaw tightened as he saw the pain rolling through Jane again.

The nurse asked for details, and Kyle listed the food and drink she'd consumed. He ran his hand across Jane's shoulders and felt tension build each time the pain charged through her.

"No one else at the party appeared ill?" the woman asked.

"No one that I saw."

"All right. That's all I need for now. I'll get her into an examining room, Mr. Conroy."

"Kyle Manning. I'm a friend."

She nodded, then gestured toward an adjacent corridor. "Follow this hall to the waiting room. Someone will let you know when you can see her." She stepped behind the wheelchair. "If there's family you need to call, a telephone is inside the waiting room."

"Thanks," Kyle said, stepping out of her way. Wanting to be with Jane, not in another room, he was tempted to flash his badge, but he pushed away the urge.

When Jane vanished behind the double doors, Kyle followed the sign to the waiting room. As always on a weekend, the room was crowded with concerned families, waiting for news. He slid into a chair, bracing his elbows on his knees, hands folded in front of him, and reviewed the evening.

Earlier in the evening, Jane had been fine, no sign of illness. It was one of those quick flu viruses or food poisoning, he was sure. He reviewed the contents of their plates. Like he'd told the nurse, he and Jane had eaten basically the same food. He felt fine. So could it be food poisoning or—?

As the thought hit him, blood hammered in his temples. *No! Dear Lord, no!* He rubbed his hand across his face, then kneaded the tension knotting in his neck. It couldn't be.

Chapter Sixteen

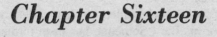

Time dragged as Kyle waited and wondered. Doctors and nurses entered and exited the waiting room, talking in soft voices to families while he stared at the door.

An hour passed, and he'd heard nothing. Earlier he'd wandered back to the admissions area, but they asked him to remain in the waiting room. "We'll let you know as soon as we can," they'd told him.

But Kyle was not good at waiting. And today he had no patience. The smell of coffee, too old and too strong, hung in the air, and frustrated, he rose and poured a cup. He returned to his chair, staring at the black brew more than drinking the potent liquid.

Another fifteen minutes passed. Finally a doctor came through the door, scanning the anxious faces, then spoke. "Family of Jane Conroy?"

Kyle jumped as if on a pulley. "I'm with Jane Conroy," he said, stepping to the doctor's side.

"Family?"

"No, a friend. We were together tonight when she got sick. Is she all right?"

"Miss Conroy has a bad case of food poisoning. We gave her an emetic to induce vomiting, then decided it was also necessary to pump her stomach. She'll have a sore throat, I'm afraid."

Fear welled in Kyle's mind. He hesitated a moment, then barreled ahead. "Look, Doctor, I'm a Redmond police officer, and I'm concerned about this. Jane has had a stalker problem."

As he spoke, Kyle pulled out his wallet and showed the doctor his ID. "Someone has been tormenting her, frightening her, at first. But I suspect the person is planning to harm her." He flipped his wallet closed and slid it back into his pocket. "Could this incident be caused by poison, rather than food poisoning?"

The doctor thought a moment. "Certainly it's possible."

"Could you have the emesis tested?"

"I'll send a sample to the lab."

Kyle felt his shoulders relax. "Thanks."

The doctor nodded. "If you'd like to see her, you can go in now. I want her to wait a few more minutes to make sure she's okay. Then you can take her home."

His mind swimming with questions, Kyle followed the doctor down the hall.

The next morning, Jane opened her eyes and pulled herself from the fog. She looked at her room. Her bed. Then she remembered the nightmare hadn't been a dream.

Confusion rattled her, and she swung her feet to the floor, trying to sort the painful memories. The nausea. The fear.

She drew a deep breath and the rich aroma of coffee beckoned her. But how?

Grabbing her robe, she hurried down the hallway, following the enticing scent and hesitated seeing Kyle sitting at her kitchen table.

He leaped up when she walked through the doorway and in a heartbeat, stood beside her. "You're okay?"

"My throat hurts," she said, feeling the raspy pain as she breathed.

"That's because they pumped your stomach."

"What are you doing here?" she asked.

"I slept on the sofa," he said, pouring her coffee.

She sat beside him, letting the warm liquid wash over her aching throat, but his concerned face pained her more deeply.

Quietly they waded through the night's events, and though he didn't say, she knew he feared the worst.

"Jane, last night, I was lost. Seeing you so ill and wondering if…and thinking how it might be…" He lowered his head and drew in a wavering breath. "I know how a woman must feel when her cop husband leaves fearing he may never came home again. But I love you. I can't lose you."

His eyes pleaded with her, and the ache settled deeper in the pit of her stomach. "Kyle, not now. We're both concerned—"

His head rose, and his gaze locked with her. "No, Jane, this is the time. You must tell me why you can't let the past go. Why are you afraid to love me?"

Could she put her feelings into words? And would he love her when he knew the truth? She drew in an uneven breath. "Years ago, Kyle, I promised myself never to fall in love with anyone even vaguely connected with the police."

"Why? Too much stress and worry?"

If that were only it. "Too much like my past. Too many bad memories." She focused on the coffee mug.

"Tell me about it, Jane. Please. Maybe saying it will ease whatever it is you're dealing with."

The role of pastor and confessor rose in her thoughts. Instead, a pastor's son would hear her confession...but only God could give her absolution.

Jane searched her thoughts. "I don't know where to begin or what's truth from fiction anymore."

"Just talk. We'll sort it out," Kyle said.

She peered into his kind, loving face, wondering if he'd feel the same when she finished.

Closing her eyes, she delved into her disorganized thoughts. "My dad was a tough man. Growing up, I saw a lot of his anger, usually vented at my mother. He brought the stress home. Nothing physical, except slamming and pounding his fist. Angry words, vile words, silence, rage. You know."

Kyle didn't respond, but his eyes remained attentive and compassionate.

Jane filled her lungs with air, released it in a quivering blast, and continued.

"Sometimes I tried to defend my mother. That's when he aimed his anger at me. He threatened me, but never hit me." She faltered. "Often, I wished he'd die."

Hesitant, she surveyed Kyle's face, fearing what she'd see. She saw only love.

Tears pooled in her eyes, and she rubbed her knuckle below each eye to catch the moisture. "I'm ashamed of that, but it's the truth. I prayed that he'd die. But I wanted God to give him a few more minutes of life…right at the very end so he'd beg for forgiveness. I thought then he'd really know how much he hurt us.''

Kyle's voice was tender. ''And did you forgive him, Jane? In your thoughts?''

''Always.'' The word quivered from her. ''But I've felt rotten facing my wishes and prayers. How can God forgive me? How can you forgive me?''

Kyle slid his hand over hers, and when he spoke, she could almost hear his father's voice. ''We pray 'Forgive us, as we forgive others.' So you're already forgiven, Jane. It's God's promise.''

''But the commandment says, 'Honor your father and mother,''' she explained, her voice raspy. ''I was angry at my father because he treated my mother badly. I broke one commandment trying to do what another says. I told lies to protect my mother—that I'd burned the chicken, that I'd broken the screen door, that I'd been home all evening when I'd been out with friends. I couldn't win.''

Kyle rose, and pulled Jane into his arms. ''Remember dad's sermon a while ago? Jesus came to earth to call *sinners,* not the righteous.''

The verse tore through Jane's mind.

''If we were perfect, Jane, would we need Jesus?'' His gaze captured hers. ''Probably not. We'd get to heaven on our own—without Jesus. But we're sinners. We all break God's law. The question is, are you sorry for your sins?''

''You know I am.'' Jane wiped the telltale tears rolling from her eyes. ''Sorrier than I could ever say.''

''Then God knows your heart. Oh, Jane, my love. He knows all our hearts.''

In her sigh, a sense of relief swept over her like cool water in a barren wasteland.

He pressed her against him, resting his cheek against her hair, and she could feel his heart beating against hers. She was surrounded by a peaceful calm.

Knowing the Christmas holiday began midweek, Jane forced herself to return to school on Monday. But more than before, she looked at her co-workers and friends with fearful eyes. Was the food poisoning really another coincidence?

When Wednesday arrived, she rushed through her classes, anxious to get away for a few days. Before she could escape the building, Jane's heart sank when she saw Skylar standing in her doorway.

As he strode into her room, he began his statement. "I was notified by central office that Mr. Malik has filed a suit against you and the district with the American Civil Liberties Union."

"A civil suit?" She rose. "Based on what?"

Skylar pursed his lips and shook his head. "You'll have to talk with Kirk Brown at central office."

"Today? Everyone's gone for the holiday, haven't they?"

"He said see him on January 4. He'll arrange for you to talk with the district's lawyers."

"I've done nothing, Mr. Skylar."

"Don't convince me. Convince the lawyers."

Civil suit. Jane's chest tightened, her breathing restricted. She couldn't imagine what Sam Malik had on his mind. Everyone knew how much she liked Lena. She looked at Skylar, realizing that nothing she could say would appease him, either.

He turned on his heel and walked out.

Jane stared at the empty doorframe. "Have a merry Christmas yourself, Mr. Skylar."

* * *

Christmas Eve day, Jane sat on the living room floor wrapping gifts. The telephone's ring made her uneasy. She hesitated to answer, but when she heard Kyle's voice, she uttered a thankful prayer. Yet the tone of his voice told her the calm would be short-lived.

"The photographs had no fingerprints. Same with the box. I'm sorry. Nothing they can do."

"It infringes on my privacy," Jane said, "and—"

"Taking photos without permission happens all the time. Think of the paparazzi."

He was right. Her mind felt packed with cotton. No room for a shred of intelligent thought.

"But you have proof now, that someone is really stalking me. The photographs prove it, don't they?"

"Right. The department kept the photos as evidence."

He left a lengthy stretch of silence. "Jane…"

Hearing his downcast voice, she froze.

"The hospital report isn't good, either."

She held her breath.

"But now we have something substantial. The results showed…you were poisoned."

He tripped on the words. They struck her like a knife, stabbing her with fear. "Poisoned. You mean *food* poisoning?" She knew the truth, but she didn't want to.

"Poisoned…isopropanol."

Breathless, she choked on the words. "But how? Who?"

"I don't know. In your food or drink."

"I ate the same things you did." Then her heart skipped a beat. "Dale gave me a pecan tart." She stared at the receiver, her mind searching for answers.

"And the chocolates. Lena gave me a box, and I ate a couple. What do you think, Kyle?"

"I don't know, Jane. Was the candy box wrapped?"

"I think so." Her memory seemed to be failing her. Too much. Too awful. Then a ray of hope brightened her thoughts. "But, Kyle, this is different. I didn't get a note this time. Nothing."

Only his deep sigh shivered through the wire.

She stared at the silent telephone until his voice made her deepest fear a reality. "If the poison had been fatal, you didn't need a note, Jane."

She sank into the chair, her limbs shaking without mercy. He was right, but she had another thought. "Kyle, there wasn't a note with the photos, either."

Silence.

"Kyle?"

Fear rose up her back as awareness struck her.

"I found a note, Jane."

His words jolted her like ice water down her back. "What...what did it say?"

He faltered. "'See Jane live?'"

She waited. That was it? "See Jane live..." *Live* wasn't frightening. *Die* was. Still, the torment went on. And what would the next note say? The receiver trembled against her cheek. "Kyle, I can't take this anymore."

"But there's a positive side to this, Jane."

"*Positive* side. What could be positive about this? Nothing." The words tore from her. Every ounce of frustration and fear sizzled through the air. "Nothing. I'm tired of living in fear. I can't stand this."

"Calm down, Jane, please."

She covered her face with her free hand, her tears running over the telephone mouthpiece. "I want to hide, run away, do anything.'' Her sobs caught in her throat. ''Dear Lord, please help me.''

''Jane, hear me out,'' he said. ''Now you have the department's attention. Poisoning someone is a crime. We have a case now. I'll pick up the box of chocolate and send them to the lab.''

His words made a slow path through her confused, frustrated mind. He was right. If she had the police's attention, it was the first good thing that had happened.

''Jane, are you okay? I'm sorry. I'm on the desk today. I should have waited until I could come over to tell you.'' His voice was filled with remorse.

''I know you meant well.'' She thought about what he had said, sending a gleam of hope into her dark thoughts. ''Having a real tangible case is good. Maybe now something can happen. I'm at the end of my patience, that's all.''

''Who could blame you?'' Silence hung on the line. Then she heard his sigh. ''I wish I could be with you tonight. I hate to leave you alone on Christmas Eve.''

''Betsy and Perry invited me for dinner, and I'm joining them for worship. I'll be fine. And Perry said he'd pick me up.''

''I'm glad. And I'll see you early tomorrow. We'll have the whole day.''

The whole day. The words caressed her ear. Yet how many Christmases had she and her mother sat alone? Too many.

She pressed the telephone into the cradle with trembling fingers. Poison. Like ice, the word left her frozen and numb. Her persecutor was not playing games. She realized that now. Someone wanted her dead.

''Hark! The herald angels sing, glory to the newborn king!'' The music echoed through the church rafters.

Last night with Betsy she couldn't rid herself of worry. Today with Kyle at her side, she felt safer, and Jane struggled to push the past months' fears from her mind and concentrate on the wonderful Christmas message.

Paul rose to deliver the sermon, and Kyle wrapped his hand in hers. His reassuring presence comforted her, and her mind cleared, giving her focus on the lesson. Here in God's house is where she could find peace, leaving her burdens at the foot of the cross. Yet, as always, Jane had to work to let go. She clung to her past like plastic wrap to a glass dish.

On her way to the Mannings' after church, Jane recalled something Betsy had said that triggered her memory—the rumors about Jane's father. The end of her senior year was disturbing, and she'd blocked out the incident that blackened her father's reputation and haunted his career. Had she recounted that situation in her diary?

After dinner, she settled with Kyle's family around the Christmas tree and unwrapped gifts. Jane was touched by Kyle's gift, a gold sculptured heart suspended from a diamond-cut gold chain.

"I'm giving you my heart," he whispered in her ear as he clasped it around her neck.

When Kyle unwrapped his navy cashmere sweater, Jane wished the gift was as romantic as the locket. But the sweater fit perfectly, and he looked handsome in it.

When all the gifts were opened and the torn tissue stuffed into a trash bag, Jane curled her legs on the sofa and sipped hot chocolate.

With Kyle nestled beside her, she fixed her gaze on the perfect Douglas fir glinting its colorful display in the dimmed lamplight. As Christmas carols played softly, the four sat in silence, enjoying the music.

Yet, in the quiet, fear edged into Jane's thoughts. The stalker had been a constant fear, but recently she'd had reoccurring questions about her and Kyle. Though she'd spent Christmas Eve with Betsy, Jane had felt alone. Loving an officer meant loneliness, worries and fears.

Every time Kyle was late, Jane would fear the worst. The concern pressed against her heart. She was torn. Loving him hurt too much, and not loving him hurt her more. Only God could solve her overwhelming predicament.

Feeling guilty, Kyle shifted and squeezed Jane's hand. He'd been withdrawn much of the evening. His mind was littered with thoughts about his future. If he'd followed his heart, Jane's Christmas gift would have been an engagement ring.

Four months—that's all they'd known each other. But four months, four years, it was all the same. It seemed he'd known her forever...and loved her even longer. But she'd been clear about her feelings. Until they resolved his career, Jane wouldn't accept his proposal. He couldn't bear to have her turn him down.

Gaining courage, Kyle eyed his father relaxing in the recliner. "Dad, have you talked any more with Walter Kitzmiller?"

His father did a double take. "No, why?" He straightened in his chair.

"I've been thinking."

With the speed of a bullet, Jane faced him. A mixture of emotions flashed across her countenance.

"Don't either of you get your hopes up." Kyle shifted his gaze like a wind sock. "I'm thinking, that's all, but I need to talk with Kitzmiller before I can make a decision.''

"I've prayed long and hard to hear you say that." Paul shifted the release on the recliner and eased forward. "And I've prayed that God keeps my mouth closed and let you handle your own life, but I'm happy you're thinking."

Struck by emotion, Kyle closed his eyes.

"Just know that whatever you decide, son, I'll stand behind you all the way. If you pray about your decision, the good Lord will tell you the way you should go."

Kyle sent him a wry smile. "I've prayed so much, the Lord's tired of hearing me."

Paul adjusted the chair to a reclining position. "He's listening. That's all you need to know."

Kyle expected Jane to let out a wild cheer as blatant as his father's beaming face, but she didn't. Instead, he saw a teary mist rimming her lashes. Her reaction confused him. He studied her silence, longing to know her mind. "So?" he asked finally.

But she stared down at her lap. "What?"

"What do you think?"

"I think we should talk later." Desperation filled her eyes.

He caressed her shoulder and felt her tense. "All right." But it wasn't all right. It was all wrong.

She nodded, but her response took the edge off his excitement. He'd hoped his sacrifice might help her understand how much he loved her.

For years, his parents hinted for him to find a safer job, but he hadn't moved. Now, for Jane, he'd give her the world. If Kitzmiller's position was anything he could tolerate, he'd take it.

Like a bullet blasting through his chest, the thought of leaving the force left a hole in his heart.

On the way home, Jane's thoughts were racing. Kyle wanted to talk, but she asked him to wait until they reached the house. Their silence sparked with tension.

Jane had struggled with her feelings all evening. She'd felt God's hand guiding her to Kyle, but the past two days had sent her in another direction. She'd been thinking only of her needs. She needed to think of Kyle's. She had to let him go.

Sorrow rose within her in chilling waves; incredible grief sat against her chest and stifled her breath. She felt lost, and more alone than ever in her life.

Inside the house, Kyle captured her in his arms. "Jane, what's wrong? You're frightening me."

"I'm sorry, Kyle. Please sit down." She motioned to a chair. "We need to talk."

"If it's the Kitzmiller thing, I didn't know what else to do. I want to make you happy." He looked confused. "I thought a new job would please you. I'm doing it for you."

"Please don't, Kyle. That's the problem. Whatever you do, do it for you."

"But we're not just you and me any longer, Jane. In my heart, we're already one. If I do something for you, it gives me pleasure. Your unhappiness is mine."

She clung to the chair arms, trying to sort her confusion. "That's where you're wrong, Kyle."

"How am I wrong? We've talked about letting God guide us. Sometimes I think we're so busy doing what we want to do we miss where the Lord's leading us. He's leading me to a new career. Don't you understand?"

"No, because I don't think it's God talking to you. It's me talking. And I'm not God. I told you from the start I can't fall in love with a police officer. But I did. And I won't let you ruin your life for me."

He buried his face in his hands. "Jane, you're making no sense. Please." He lifted his head and torment filled his face.

Jane's heart sank to unknown depths. She had to stay strong for him. "It makes all the sense in the world. I want you to be happy. You love being a police officer. I can't allow you to quit the force for me."

"Stop it, Jane. It's for us."

"It's your life, Kyle. Not mine. Please. Please, go." Her sigh rattled through her like dry bones.

Kyle's face filled with disbelief. He rose from the chair, and without turning back, he walked out the door.

Jane caved into the sofa, filled with unspeakable grief.

Three days after Christmas, the telephone rang. When Jane heard the sound of Paul's voice, she knew.

"Kyle's been shot, Jane."

"Oh, please Lord, no." A moan tore from her throat. A dizzying sensation swooped over her, and she caught the edge of the kitchen counter to keep from crumbling to the floor.

"Are you okay, Jane?"

She closed her eyes, pushing the tears back, her voice a faint whisper. "Yes, I'm...I'm.... Is he—"

"He's wounded, but alive, thank God. They're taking him in for surgery now."

"He's alive?" An image of Kyle lying in a pool of

blood shivered through her mind. Her throat ached from repressing her tears.

"Yes. A bullet in the shoulder, they said. We're headed for Redmond Community Hospital now."

Jane clung to the counter, nausea sweeping through her. "I'm coming, too." *Please, God. Please.*

"We'll pick you up," Paul said.

"No, I'm okay. You go ahead, and I'll be there as quickly as I can."

"But—"

She steadied her voice. "I'm fine."

"Be careful, Jane. The roads are slick. Really wet and icy. Are you sure—"

"Yes, please, go ahead. Kyle needs you. I'll be there as soon as I can."

Jane dropped the phone and covered her face. Tears rolled down her cheeks while guilt and sorrow washed over her heart. She hadn't listened to God. Her own frailty had sent Kyle away. For the past three days, she'd suffered and struggled with her foolish decision. She needed—no, longed—to beg Kyle's forgiveness.

Trembling uncontrollably, Jane hurried outside and understood Paul's concern. The steps were glazed with ice, and she inched her way to the car.

After starting the engine, she turned on the heater, then grabbed the scraper and chiseled ice from the windshield. Climbing inside, the engine had warmed, and she shifted into reverse and backed from the driveway.

Her body trembled as a desperate weakness spread through her limbs. No longer could she worry about herself. Getting to the hospital and to Kyle pushed her beyond common sense. She clung to the wheel, feeling the tires slide at each pump of the brake.

On the highway, the salt trucks had dumped their wares on the cement, but the tires still skated beneath her. Jane spoke aloud, lifting her worries in prayer and begging God to make things right. Tonight she needed to hang on and let the Lord guide her.

A lonely stretch of highway loomed before her, and she glanced in the rearview mirror. A car crept behind her, dangerously close. Certainly the driver should stay back. But the car edged forward.

Fearful, Jane pressed on the gas pedal, her tires slipping on the treacherous surface. Her pulse raced. With a death grip on the wheel, she focused on the highway. She had to reach Kyle safely. In the mirror, the car moved steadily toward her bumper.

Why would some fool be speeding on this treacherous road? Her legs turned to gelatin; her foot felt powerless against the pedal. The other car shot forward—too close, and when the driver hit the high beams, the glare in her rearview mirror blinded her. In panic, she adjusted the mirror with shaking fingers.

Jane caught a reflection in the side mirror. The car pulled forward, passing her on the left, sliding toward her, closing the distance between them. Her heart hammered in her throat.

Her sedan veered off the highway.

Chapter Seventeen

As Jane's car slid out of control, the deep ditch loomed out of the darkness and a metal guardrail clipped her bumper. She clung to the wheel, spinning sideways, then skidded to a stop on the shoulder. Panic screamed in her ears.

The other vehicle shot past, sliding to a stop. The car's back-up lights brightened, and Jane sat in frozen terror. Was the driver stopping to help or was it...? *Lord, what should I do?* Jump out? Run?

Answering her prayer, a pair of headlights glowed in her rearview mirror. In a heartbeat, the other car changed gears and sped off into the night. Behind her, the car slowed and pulled off the road. Her body trembled. Her lungs burned. Tears dripped from her chin.

A tap hit her driver's side window. She cringed as a faint voice sounded through the glass. "Are you okay?"

Hesitant, she lowered the window an inch, and the young man repeated his question. "Are you all right? That car ran you off the road."

She nodded. "I'm okay."

He stepped back, looked at the situation, then returned and squinted through the gap in her window. "Listen, just step lightly on the gas pedal. Lightly, but firmly. Don't gun it. Understand?"

She nodded.

"Real steady," he said. "If she slides, then raise your foot."

Swallowing her emotions, Jane reviewed his instructions. She pushed lightly on the pedal, but the wheels spun.

She eased back, then tried again. This time the tires gripped and rolled forward.

The man motioned toward the road, his voice calling above the engine. "Don't stop. Just keep going."

Jane steered back to the cement and down the highway, watching his silhouette fade against his headlights. Prayers of thanksgiving rose to heaven, and she tried to calm her runaway heart. An accident, that's all it was. Tonight she had no one to turn to—no one who understood like Kyle. Why had she sent him away?

The hospital lights glowed in the distance. Jane used the emergency entrance, gained parking and entered the surgical waiting room.

Kyle's parents weren't there. Her breathing faltered. Was something wrong? She turned and rushed down the corridor to the E.R. nurses' station.

"Kyle Manning," she said, her voice breathless.

The woman checked the clipboard and gestured through the double doors. "Curtain ten," she said.

Jane pushed through the doorway. Paul and Ruth stood alone outside the curtained room. Jane crumbled into Paul's arms, allowing her emotions free reign. "How's Kyle?" she asked through her tears.

Ruth smiled with red-rimmed eyes. "They're getting him ready for surgery."

Paul patted Ruth's shoulder. "The surgeon talked with us. It'll take at least an hour, he said."

Jane viewed his parents' worried faces, and her heart ached for them as much as herself. They'd already lost one son. They couldn't lose another. "Can we see him?"

"She's giving him a shot, to relax him I guess," Ruth murmured. "Then we can go back in until…"

Paul moved his hand in soothing circles on Ruth's back. "We joined in prayer with Kyle, didn't we, Mama?"

Daubing her eyes, Ruth murmured, "Yes."

The curtain slid back, and the nurse stepped past them without looking. "You can go back in," she said.

Though she longed to run through the doorway, Jane held back, allowing the Mannings to enter first. But when she stepped inside, his parents pushed her ahead. Her heart stood still.

Covered by a hospital gown, Kyle's large frame filled the gurney. She ached seeing him helpless. He was her guardian, her knight in blue. Jane eyed his shoulder covered with a thick bloodstained bandage. Her stomach churned, and she pulled her focus from the wound. What could she do to let Kyle know she loved him?

"If it isn't Redmond's finest," she said, struggling to keep her voice steady and her tears harnessed.

"Not today," he said, a grimace wavering across his face. He reached across the white blanket to capture her trembling hand.

Her spirit lifted while guilt tugged it back down. "What happened?"

He coughed, wincing as the pain wrenched through him. "The same two...another holdup."

Kyle's eyelids drooped, but he wrestled them open. "George and I answered the backup call." He drew a deep breath and flinched. "That's when the shooting began."

Ruth clung to the bed rail. "Praise the Lord, another squad car showed up to help them."

"Kyle said they were just young fellows." Paul shook his head. "Such a pity."

"George?" Jane asked. "Is he all right?"

"He's fine," Paul said. "He'll try to stop by after he files the report."

"He left a message at the desk," Ruth added. "Such a nice man."

When Jane turned back to Kyle, his eyes were closed, and his deep breathing alerted her that the anesthetic had begun to work. Seeing him so vulnerable, she was struck by the truth. What would she do without Kyle? He was everything. Her life. Her old fears gave a tug. Forget the past, a powerful voice resounded inside her.

Before she collected her thoughts, the curtain was drawn back and an orderly stepped in to wheel him away.

She stood with Kyle's parents, watching the gurney until it turned the corner. Then Paul steered them back out the double door to the waiting room.

As they sat, silence fell over them. The quiet voice inside her had spoken. The Lord had spoken. She would forget the past and let God be in charge.

Her frightening ride spun in her thoughts, but she pushed it aside. If she had good sense, she would have noted the license plate number. She couldn't remember a thing. Not the car's make or color. Nothing.

Eventually they talked, anything to fill the waiting, and time passed. They said nothing about her quarrel with Kyle. Were they being kind or hadn't Kyle told them? With each movement at the door, Jane raised her head, then lowered it again. Tension grew until she felt tears edging from her eyes again. She pulled a tissue from her handbag, wiping the moisture that rolled down her cheeks.

Paul shifted in his chair and placed his hand on her arm. "Let's pray together, Jane. This waiting is unbearable." He extended his hand toward her.

She looked into Paul's kind, misted eyes and grasped his strong hand, feeling safe for the first time since his telephone call. Ruth clasped the other, and they bowed their heads as Paul prayed aloud for Kyle's safety and their peace and understanding.

As she listened to his comforting words, tears fell to her lap. All the misery she'd felt for weeks—maybe a lifetime—drained from her. Ruth and Paul's strong faith wrapped her like a cocoon and uplifted her.

Would her life have been different if she'd known this fatherly man years ago when she was an unhappy teenager? Jane ached, remembering how she wanted to love her own father—and she did, but her love was troubled and confused.

When Paul released her hand, he patted her arm. "Feel better?" His eyes were hopeful.

"Yes," she said. "Thanks."

Paul's expression changed, and Jane followed his attention toward the doorway. A surgeon stood in the entrance, gowned in green. He nodded and joined them.

Watching him stride across the room, Jane clutched her trembling hands. But Paul's prayer clung to her memory, and eyeing the doctor's confident face, Jane's spirits lifted.

"The surgery went well," the doctor said. "He'll have a bad shoulder for a while, and he'll need to strengthen those damaged muscles, but everything's fine."

"Praise the Lord. Thank you," Ruth murmured.

"Can we see him?" Paul asked.

Jane longed to ask the same question, but it didn't seem her place. Not yet.

"He's in recovery now. You can see him for a minute when he's in a room. Tomorrow he'll be better company. Now he needs rest." He squeezed Paul's shoulder. "They'll let you know when you can go in."

Paul nodded, and as the surgeon retreated through the doorway, Paul steered them toward the exit. "We have at least an hour, so let's go for coffee and, maybe, a little dessert. Then we'll come back and wait."

They agreed, and when they were settled in the cafeteria, the women sipped coffee while Paul ate a piece of pie. They spoke about the Christmas holiday, anything to keep their minds off their worries.

But Jane's mind overflowed with the stress of her past weeks. Unbidden, she released a troubled sigh. "I feel so lost without Kyle. He's the one I turn to."

"Don't forget the Lord," Paul said, knitting his fingers together on the table.

Reality coursed through her. She'd let the Lord fade from her life, and now, letting God back in was a struggle. How long had she leaned on herself rather than God? And where had it gotten her? Nowhere. Only more hurt and heartache.

"You've both been so kind to me."

"The feeling is mutual," Ruth said. "You've been a blessing to us."

Jane's eyes pooled with tears. Ruth was a true pastor's wife—gentle, compassionate, and always supporting her husband. How could Jane ever support Kyle's career in that way? Today was a prime example of a future with him. Fear. Loneliness. Yet she loved him too much to let him go. The paradox was mind-boggling.

Paul studied her face. "You love Kyle, don't you?"

His question hit her like a punch in the solar plexis. Yes. She did, but it was so much more complex than a plain "yes." The words wouldn't come, but she nodded.

She stared at the cup in front of her, studied the greasy glaze shining from the too-strong coffee.

"You see your father's career in Kyle's. Is that right?" Paul asked.

She nodded.

"Faith, Jane. That's what we all need. Good strong faith. I speak for myself…and Ruth. We need to put those fears in God's hands."

He was right. Unable to speak, Jane prayed, and when she had calmed, she glanced at her wristwatch.

Giving her hand a pat, Paul rose. "Time to get back."

Jane nodded, wishing she could tell him more.

Paul helped Ruth, then Jane, from their chairs.

Standing beside him, Jane imagined how Kyle would look years from now. Handsome, strong, with little wisps of gray in his trim brown hair. She stretched on tiptoe and kissed Paul's cheek while her heart stretched toward heaven.

* * *

When they returned to the waiting room, Kyle's nurse was just leaving. "No more than two at a time," she said. "And please keep your visits short for today. He's still groggy and needs rest."

She motioned for them to follow, but Jane held back indicating that they should go first. Paul looked at her with questioning eyes, but Jane insisted.

When they were gone, she slumped into the nearest chair and bowed her head, praying for Kyle's recovery, and in the waiting silence, she prayed she might learn to put all her cares in God's hands.

As she sorted her wavering thoughts, Paul came to the door and beckoned. He guided her down the hall, then left her with Ruth.

Jane hesitated in the doorway, surveying the room with relief—only one IV bottle and a single monitor blipping Kyle's vital signs. No other fearful, high-powered machines loaded with bells and whistles stood beside Kyle's bed.

Ruth's strained face had relaxed, and she motioned for Jane to join her. At the foot of the bed, Jane ached, seeing Kyle still and silent. His eyes were closed, his shoulder bound with thick, gauzy cloth and heavy tape.

"He's still sleeping," Ruth whispered, but as she spoke, his eyelids flickered, then closed again. Ruth's face brightened, and she leaned down and kissed his forehead. His lids fluttered again, and Jane heard an incoherent murmur.

"He called me Mom," Ruth said, her face glowing. "Come closer, Jane. Talk to him."

Jane moved to Kyle's side, slid her palm over his still hand, then bent closer to his ear. "Hey, Redmond's finest," she murmured. "How are you doing?"

His hand shifted, and his lids flickered open again. "Hi, Jackson's finest," he muttered, his voice thick.

Her heart skipped, and despite Ruth watching, she placed a gentle kiss on his parched lips.

He struggled to focus, and beneath her hand, one of his fingers caught hers. His mouth formed soundless words, but she read the beautiful message on his lips. "I love you."

Thin rivulets of tears rolled down her cheeks. With her free hand, she brushed them away. "Kyle, I love you. Do you hear me? I love you." Finally she'd said the words. Three small words. One mammoth commitment.

An escaped tear dripped from her chin and dropped to Kyle's hand. "I'll hold you to that," he whispered.

"You're going to be fine, Kyle. Now, you need to rest," Jane said. "I'll let your dad come back, and I'll see you tomorrow."

He gave her an indistinct nod, and she pressed his hand a final time before letting go.

Paul insisted she wait, and after their parting with Kyle, he and Ruth walked with her to the parking lot. After saying good night, she opened her car door and slid inside, then gasped, noticing the paper caught beneath the passenger windshield wiper.

Her stomach cramped as a wave of nausea rolled through her. Peering into the darkness, she scanned the parking lot. Terror tore at her confidence. She didn't want to look. If she turned on the wipers, she could let it fly away into the winter wind, the message unread.

The Mannings' car vanished into the night, and Jane, watching it go, felt empty and alone. Fear dueled with anger, lashing her to the seat cushion. Fighting her panic, she slid from the car, yanked the note from the wiper and darted to safety, plunging down the door locks.

She turned on the ignition and, in the dashboard's glow, unfolded the paper. The note confirmed her worst fear. Her earlier scare had been no accident.

Look! Look! Look! See Jane skid.

Chapter Eighteen

The next day, Jane went to the hospital early, but Paul was already there, sitting at Kyle's side, reading the Bible while his son slept.

He rose and pulled another chair beside his. They talked softly and waited. Jane longed to tell Paul about her frightening experience. But telling anyone seemed useless, and if Kyle overheard, he would only be more frustrated. She swallowed her desire. She'd tell him after he was well.

Kyle moaned faintly, then opened his eyes.

"Good morning," she said.

"Am I in heaven?" he asked, his voice stronger. "I see an angel." He grinned.

His smile filled her. He still loved her. As if God touched her, she sensed things would be all right.

His father laughed. "Heaven on earth, maybe. You feeling better?"

"I'm hungry."

Jane's spirit lifted. Hunger was a good sign. She

rolled his tray of uneaten breakfast to his bed, lifted the lids and returned to the chair.

Kyle delved into the food. "Have you been here all night?" he asked. He caught a stray piece of cold toast with his napkin.

Paul laughed. "We walked her to the parking lot last night and forced her to leave."

"That true?" Kyle asked.

Jane nodded, her pulse skipping when she thought of the parking lot.

He stretched his arm toward her. "A long, boring evening."

"Long, but not boring. Your dad gave me something to think about," Jane said, taking his hand and moving to his side.

"Is that good or bad?" Kyle said, giving her a tired grin.

"Good," she said. "You know how I've felt about my dad."

He nodded and squeezed her hand.

"Jane," Paul said, his face strained, "I've been thinking and, well, maybe…I can help you more than I have. I, eh, know a lot of things about your dad."

She jerked her head toward him. "I don't understand," she said, controlling her panic.

"It's a long, troubling story, but your dad and I knew each other more than just those committees I mentioned before. I don't have to protect anyone any longer…I don't think. Tell me what's really bothering you, Jane."

After so many years, how could she explain her true feelings? She wasn't sure *she* knew what they were. She'd lived in distorted recollections and guilty memories so long, her reality and fantasy had tangled. She sorted her thoughts. "I suppose the worst were the rumors and threats."

"You heard rumors?" Paul asked, his brows knitting. "And you were threatened?

She nodded. "Rumors that Dad was mixed up in the rackets. I was ashamed to think my dad was a crooked cop, but when he was killed, I was sure they were true."

Paul's face contorted, sending a haunting feeling skittering through Jane.

"But they weren't true," Paul said. "I know."

Jane's head snapped upward. She peered at him, waiting to hear anything that might help her understand.

Kyle squeezed Jane's hand. "Explain, Dad."

"Your father let the rumors live, trying to protect someone."

Her pulse coursed through her veins. "He what?"

"He took the heat off someone else...or tried to."

Kyle nodded knowingly, but Jane searched Paul's face, not understanding.

"That's the long story I mentioned."

Jane eyed Kyle, then Paul. "I'd like to know...."

Paul drew in a lengthy breath and leaned forward, elbows on his knees, hands folded. "A man walked into the church one day years ago and asked if we could talk. He was involved in the rackets—drugs and money laundering. He wanted out. But he was scared to death."

Kyle scowled. "A church member?"

"No. I never saw him before."

"Why did he come to you?" Jane asked.

"No idea. He may have lived in the area. Who

knows? I contacted the police and worked out a deal for him. It was your dad who came to the church.''

The story rolled through her. ''You mean the man confessed to my dad?''

''Ratted is what they call it,'' Kyle said.

Paul nodded. ''They promised him immunity for information. The vice squad wanted the big guys. You know, the kingpins.''

Jane drank in the story, facts she wished she'd heard years earlier. ''And did they get the…kingpins?''

''Some of them. Eventually.''

Her heart tripped. ''But the rumors…about my father?''

''When the police got busy, the journalists got nosy, pressing for the name of the stoolie. Your dad took the brunt of their guessing game. They knew he was involved somehow.''

Jane's hands trembled in Kyle's. For the first time, she understood. ''So the police made up a story?''

''Yes. If they didn't have a stoolie, then they needed a crooked cop. Redmond had some, I'm sure, but not your dad.'' He stared directly into her eyes. ''Do you understand?''

Jane nodded.

''But your father didn't deny it. It would have put the informant in danger…or me, Jane. He kept his mouth shut.''

''Is that why my dad was shot?'' she asked.

''I can only guess. I think there was a connection.''

Agony seemed to fill his face, and he caved against the chair back. Though Jane wanted to stop, she needed to hear the truth.

With a heavy sigh, Paul continued. ''Your dad knew

too much for his own good. It was too late for the mob to shut him up. But they could get even.''

Blood hummed in her ears. She caught her breath. ''Like a vendetta?''

''That's what I think,'' Paul said.

''Sure sounds like it,'' Kyle agreed.

Guilt and sorrow surfaced on Paul's strained face.

''And they never knew about you?'' Jane asked.

Fidgeting, he closed his eyes for a moment, then pressed his hands together in fists and shook his head.

''God is good,'' Jane said. ''I'm grateful.'' She slid her hand over his knotted fingers. ''What about the other guy? The informant?''

''Dead.''

''They killed him, too?'' Jane understood the hidden sorrow Paul had carried for so many years and wished she hadn't riled the stagnant waters of his memories.

''But not before the department had all the facts they needed,'' Paul said.

''I'm sorry I made you remember it all. I had no idea.''

''If it helps you, then it's worth it,'' he said.

The reality of his words rose around her like ice on her sprain. Slowly the cooling impact of his words soothed and comforted her. ''My dad was innocent.''

Paul touched her arm. ''He was a good cop, Jane.''

''His only sin was a bad temper,'' she whispered.

A faint look of amusement flickered on Paul's face. ''Well, I wouldn't know about the *only* sin. But I imagine he was a regular sinner like all of us.''

She nodded, squeezing her eyes together to control the sobs that lay like a knot in her throat.

''You're a good woman,'' he added. ''You've been

punishing yourself for what you thought were your dad's sins.''

She looked at him through a blur of tears. ''I have, I guess.''

''The Bible says something that I wish you'd recalled years ago. 'Fathers shall not be put to death for their children, nor children put to death for their fathers; each is to die for his own sin.' You remember that now.''

''I will.''

''That's good,'' he said.

Kyle released a heavy sigh. ''Does Mom know about this?''

''She sure does,'' his father said. ''I never keep anything from your mother.''

Jane listened, lost in thought. Her father was a hero, and she'd believed all those years he'd been a bad cop. The news washed over her like a balm. Her dad had still been an angry man, too vile at times and too quick to rant at her mother, but now the knowledge added a new spin to the story. It had taken the edge off, softened it as if the bright interrogation lights were dimmed. Now, for the first time, Jane saw a human being beneath the burning glare—her father.

And Paul was right. In judging her father, she had also judged herself. She had tried to bear his sins, as well as her guilt, and they had weighted her down. Her vision turned to the church window, the picture of the wounded Christ bearing the sins of the world, and she wished she'd given her weighty load to the Lord long ago.

On New Year's Eve day, Kyle stretched out on his parents' sofa, dressed in sweatpants and shirt. Using wisdom, he'd agreed to spend a few days with them, recuperating. He was frustrated, though, and anxious for some privacy with Jane. He longed to know if the new information about her father would make a difference.

When his mother opened the door, he heard Jane's voice. She bounded into the living room, and he was glad when his mother made an excuse, leaving them alone.

Kyle sat up, eased his left shoulder into the sofa corner and reached for Jane with his right arm. She rushed into his embrace.

"I've missed you," he said, nuzzling his chin against her soft, fragrant hair. "Never thought a woman could wrap me around her tiny finger, but you have."

"Kyle, I'm sorry. I have no excuse and nothing to say, except I love you, and I beg you to forgive me."

"Nothing to forgive, Jane. I forgave you the moment I walked out the door. I just waited for you to tell me to come home."

"Come home," she said, tears wetting her lashes.

He caressed her smooth cheek, then let his kisses trail from her forehead to her nose, kissed the dampness from her eyes and ended where he longed to be—her lips.

The kiss sent a trail of longing down his limbs. Yet, against his wishes, a new awareness surged. She had spoken the words he'd wanted to hear—*I love you*. But with his fears, could he handle her love?

His eyes lingered over each detail of her face until, filled with desire, he lowered his mouth to hers, deepening the kiss.

He felt her excitement, yielding to his touch.

With a final caress, Kyle released her and said the

words on his mind. "Before I met you, I prayed each time I went to work that I'd come home in one piece. Now I have someone to come home for, and life seems too precious. I'm...not sure I want to put you through these fears every day."

The thought of losing her reared in his mind, and he pressed her torso against his right shoulder, holding her as if she might vanish if he let her go.

"I don't have answers, Kyle, but I don't want to lose you," she whispered in his ear. "I'll accept anything you decide to do with your life—our life." She ran her hand along his jaw, raising one finger and pressing it against his lips. "Please don't say anything. Not now."

She slid her hand to the nape of his neck and he felt his muscles flex with her touch. He wanted her more than he could say, but how? How could he resolve the fears that tore at him. His badge stood between them. His parents' pleading faces filled his mind. Would he see the same frightened look in Jane's?

Though she'd learned more about her father—about the past that hurt her so deeply—Kyle faced the truth. He could only offer her the same life. Without the violence, maybe, but the same day-in and day-out danger, never knowing when or where he might be gunned down.

He winced at his throbbing wound beneath the thick bandage. He released his grip on Jane, trying to relax the tension in his shoulders.

Her face echoed the same mixed emotions he felt. Fear, longing, desperation.

She lifted his hand and kissed his fingers. "In the past months, I've felt more complete with you than I have my entire life."

The feeling was his own. Kyle brushed his lips

against her ear, pushing away the worry that nagged at him. He hoped that prayer and time would give him insight. "You nabbed my heart the first day I saw you…and without reading me my rights."

"You have no rights when it comes to me."

He caught hold of her teasing, and let it pull him from his worries. "I'm just a prisoner of love."

As Kyle's voice faded, his mother returned to the room, ending their private talk. "Your dad's pulling in," she said to Kyle. "So dinner won't be too long. I've set a place for you, Jane, and don't say a word." She offered a warm smile and lifted a cautioning finger.

Jane did as she was told. The only word she uttered was a quiet prayer, thanking God for this loving family.

On January fourth, Jane left the central office building, feeling that someone finally understood the situation with Sam Malik better than Skylar did. She'd reviewed the situation with the administration, and she would meet the school district's lawyers and someone from the American Civil Liberties Union.

A few days later, she sat surrounded by lawyers, Kirk Brown and legal people from the ACLU. She'd gone over her story and was surprised to learn they had already talked with parents, staff and students in their investigation.

To her surprise, Sam Malik's charge was the opposite of what she had imagined. His suit claimed Lena suffered embarrassment and discrimination by receiving special ed support when no proven learning disabilities existed. His scheme was a hoax for money, and she'd fallen prey.

With testimony from others, she was assured that

she'd be cleared of any civil rights charges. Jane left the meeting with relief.

When she arrived home, a Happy Birthday balloon sat on her front porch attached to a package. She grinned. Kyle had been teasing her about her impending thirtieth birthday. Feeling the weight of the package, she figured he'd elicited George's help in getting it to the house.

Scooting it through the front door, the package felt like bricks. She dropped her coat and bag on the chair and pulled off the box wrappings. The balloon floated to the ceiling before she could nab the string. She pulled off the card taped to the box, and her blood froze. The simple message said, "Happy birthday, Jane." But the block print looked all too familiar.

With her heart as heavy as the gift, she stared at the dismal box. If it had been a bomb, she'd already be blown to smithereens since she'd jiggled the package while carrying it inside by herself. But fearful, and sickened by the situation, she hesitated to open it.

Finally she made her decision. She hurried to the telephone and, with shaking fingers, dialed. Kyle would tell her what to do.

But Ruth answered. "Kyle's not here, Jane." Ruth hesitated. "Is something wrong?"

Hoping she wouldn't upset Kyle's mother, she explained briefly. "I thought he'd tell me what to do," Jane said. "I'm sure it's nothing, but—"

"Don't touch it, Jane. Paul's here. Let me put him on the line."

Within moments, Paul answered. "Hold on, Jane. I'll be there in a few minutes."

After giving Paul her address, Jane hung up, stared at the ominous box, and waited.

When she heard the car pull into the driveway, Jane flung open the door and her heart soared when she saw Kyle. The tension tearing through her had reached its peak, and she threw herself into his embrace.

Seeing Jane's fear, Kyle ached and held her tightly against his chest, eyeing the box near the foyer doorway. When her trembling subsided, he eased her back and kissed her hair.

She scowled. "I thought you were—"

"Dad was just leaving when I got home, so I came instead." He'd known something was very wrong when he'd looked at his father's face.

"I'm glad."

"So you're thinking this isn't a surprise birthday gift, huh?" he asked, trying to make light of the situation.

"No, I'm sure it's not. My birthday's Wednesday, but look at the note. It's like the others."

Kyle took the paper and studied the note, then slid the message back into her hand and knelt beside the box. "I suppose the only way we'll know what's inside is to open it."

Though he planted a casual look on his face, inside he seethed with anger and frustration. He drew a pocket knife through the wide packaging tape and eyed Jane's shaking limbs as she backed to the sofa and sat.

"Good," Kyle said, glancing at her, "now, stay back." He tore at the cardboard and lifted the lid. He peered inside, tipping the box one way and then the other. "It's a cement block. That's it."

She rose and leaned above him, bracing her trembling hand against his back. "Are you sure?"

"Positive." He reached in and pulled out a gray concrete block. "I don't know what to think."

He rolled the block over to reveal a piece of paper. His mind flew, staring at the ominous numbers. A date? House number? Code?

Jane eyed the note. "Looks like a lock combination." He leaned forward. "5 5:9. Is that what you see?"

Frustrated, he returned the block to the carton, then sat on a chair and stared at the box. "Could I see that note again?"

Jane handed him the slip of paper, and he stared at it silently. The marks meant something. Some kind of clue, but he didn't get it.

"I'll have someone from the Precinct pick up the block, Jane, but I'll take the note with me. I don't understand the message at all."

"Take it, please," Jane said. "I don't want to look at the package or the note."

He rose and dropped the newest note into his pocket, knowing he had to speak about another issue. "I want you to know I went for the Kitzmiller interview."

"That's where you were?"

"You told me to do what I was led to do, right?"

Jane nodded, but he saw the sadness in her face.

How could he make her understand he had to do this for her? It was his sacrifice.

Chapter Nineteen

"**H**appy birthday to you. Happy birthday to you."

Kyle and his parents circled Jane as Ruth held the candle-lit birthday cake. The woman had overwhelmed Jane with the special birthday dinner and now the cake.

Kyle grinned at her, his wounded arm resting on a bookshelf. "Make a wish, Jane."

Here first thought was the stalker. "You all know my wish. It's not a secret." But Kyle's handsome face rose in her vision, and her heart two-stepped. She smiled. "But I have another one I can make." She closed her eyes and blew out the thirty candles.

Kyle chuckled. "Takes a lot of air to blow out thirty of those babies."

Ruth held the cake in one hand and swatted at him with the other. "Now, you leave this poor girl alone. We all wish we were only thirty."

Kyle winked and brushed Jane's cheek with a kiss.

Ruth sliced the cake and poured coffee, and when the dessert was eaten, Paul rose and cleared his throat.

His expression caused fear to skitter down Jane's

back, stopping her in midconversation. Her smile faded.

"I hate to ruin the celebration, but this morning, I believe I figured out the numbers on the paper with the cement block."

Kyle brushed Jane's arm. "I showed Dad the note when I got it home."

A weakness washed over her, and from Kyle's look, she knew her face had paled. She clutched her hands into a knot on the lace tablecloth and waited.

"What caught my eye after I studied it was the colon between the numbers," Paul said.

Jane scowled. "Colon?"

"I missed that," Kyle said.

Paul continued. "A pastor immediately sees a scripture reading. When I opened the Bible, I decided the first number five had to be a book. Either Deuteronomy or Acts. So I looked at the Old Testament first. Deuteronomy 5:9. I didn't need to look further."

"What is it, Dad?" Kyle asked before Jane could.

Paul lifted the Bible from the buffet and turned to the page. "'I am a jealous God, punishing the children for the sins of the fathers.'" He looked at Jane. "It's someone from your past, Jane. Someone who knew your father. I have that feeling."

Jane felt nailed to the chair. Icy blood ran through her body. "But...I—I just don't get it. Who would punish me for the sins of my father?" She leaned toward Paul. "You told me my dad was a good cop. For years, I thought he'd been mixed up in the rackets, but you convinced me he wasn't."

"Remember, the newspaper accounts indicated otherwise," Paul reminded her. "That was part of the cover-up. Other than the police department, I was one of the only people who knew the true story.''

"So this might be a...what?'' Kyle asked. ''A relative or friend of someone looking for revenge?'' The cement block crashed into his thoughts. Revenge? What did it mean?

Paul pinched his bottom lip. ''A child of someone, someone seeking revenge for a parent. Maybe, someone prosecuted during the big scandal. I don't know.''

Kyle nodded. ''It makes sense, Dad.''

Jane stared into space, trying to piece together the puzzle. ''I guess it makes sense. Someone's trying to make me suffer like they've suffered over the years.''

"I think so,'' Paul agreed. ''Something like that.''

Jane shook her head. ''But who?''

When she arrived home from work the next day, her mind plowed through the situation as she ate dinner. Malik seemed off her list of suspects. And now she had somewhere to focus her thinking, on the ''sins of her father.'' Fear ran through her again as she struggled to swallow her food.

After dinner, she dragged out the last two diaries. She pored through one, then grasped the final book. She opened it, tossing the key on the table, and leaned back. ''January 1. Happy New Year. I graduate this year and then off to college.'' She scanned the page and turned to the next. On and on. She'd grown less naive in her comments, but so much seemed routine, day-to-day activities. Little else.

As her eyes grew heavy, Jane squinted at the blurring words, and she started to close the book. But a reference to her father jumped from the page, and she stopped herself.

As she read, memories returned. The diary recalled threats to her family that occurred late in her senior year. As far as she could calculate, the time and situation coordinated with the crime that Kyle's father told her about.

If she and her mother had been threatened at that time, could these threats be related? She read the pages again, skimming on until she read no more references to the situation. But she faltered, stumbling over the entry for the day her father was killed. Those horrible months arched and struck like a cobra in her memory.

When Kyle arrived, she handed him the diary. The tiny journal looked small in his large hand as he tucked it in his pocket. She sighed. "Maybe you can make some sense out of it."

Kyle wondered, and his heart stirred. Fear had lived in her eyes since the cider mill incident, the day they realized the stalker events weren't coincidental.

"Come here," he said, taking her in his arms. "First, I'll talk to Dad, then I'll look back in the files on that case, too. If we can find one connection from that time to now, it's a beginning."

"Beginning of the end," she said. "I can't bear much more."

"I know, and you deserve better."

She deserved more than he could say, and his heart filled with a mixture of relief and sadness, knowing he could give her better. "I want to accept the administrative position Kitzmiller offered me."

He tried to read her eyes, but whether he saw relief or sadness in her face, he wasn't sure.

"No, you can't."

Her words shocked him.

"I know you're doing it for me," she said, "but I

don't know how I can let you. You love your work. Someday you may resent it. It would come between us."

Nothing could ever come between them, his reason said, but his heart thundered with her comment. "I love you too much to lose you. I prayed, and I can do it.

He shifted and grasped her by the shoulders. "You know, Jane, changing jobs will make my folks happy, too. You've heard them. The Bible says to honor parents, and I went against my dad's wishes for my own needs. Maybe it's time to do some sacrificing for the people I love."

He lowered his mouth to hers, and her lips eagerly joined his. In that moment, Kyle tasted the joy of sacrifice for the woman he'd grown to love so deeply.

When they drew apart, Jane raised her eyes to his, and he witnessed a sacrifice of her own.

"Please, don't make any rash decisions right now," she pleaded. "Let's wait until this terrible situation is over. Please. In a couple of days you're returning to work, and I feel safe knowing you're there. Once this is settled, then we can talk. I'll think more clearly then. Please wait a little. For me."

He didn't understand. For so long, she'd been vehement about his work. Yet today her eyes begged him, and he knew she meant what she said.

"I'll wait, Jane. But I have to give Kitzmiller an answer soon. I can't hold off too long."

"Just a little while. We're making some headway. Just until this terror is over, and then we can talk."

Jane stared out the living room window as the snow fell in heavy flakes. Her trembling hand rested on the telephone and she wondered what to do. Three times the phone had rung, and when she answered, no one spoke..

Now that Kyle was back to work, she'd felt more at peace. He promised to follow any lead he could find. He'd gone over the story with his dad and scavenged the files. Tonight he said he'd stop by if he had time. Yet if the bad weather kept up, she knew that would be impossible. Too many motorist problems.

When the telephone rang again, she jumped. I won't answer. But after the fourth ring, she thought of Kyle, and hesitantly picked up the receiver.

"Hello."

An open line, but silence. Dead silence.

She slammed the receiver back on the cradle and went to the kitchen. Cocoa was soothing, and she needed something to calm her. Jane mixed hot water with instant chocolate in a thick mug, then returned to the living room and snapped on the television.

An alert ran along the bottom of the screen warning motorists of unsafe driving conditions. No question she wouldn't hear from Kyle tonight. She grabbed up a magazine, and with one eye on the TV, scanned the glossy pages.

With the winter sun hidden by heavy cloud cover, darkness had fallen around five o'clock. Jane faced a long, lonely evening. Friday night without Kyle dragged. She should have called Celia or maybe Betsy.

Thinking of Celia, she recalled that her friend had been quiet the past couple of days. But that was Celia's way—unless the news was exciting. She kept troubles to herself. Rather than think of her own worries, Jane let her mind wander through Celia's situation.

But when a thud sounded against the house, her heart rose in her throat. She ran to the front window and flashed on the porch light. Nothing. No car in the drive. She dashed on wobbling legs to the kitchen and checked the back door lock, then headed for the side window. Nothing but darkness.

Another noise came from the side of the house. Icy chills rose in prickles on her skin. She rushed to the light switch and snapped it off, then peered out the back window.

She needed a strategy. Sliding her hand up the wall, Jane snapped on the porch light. A fleeting shadow fell across the white snow, then vanished. Her heart thudded, and a wave of dizziness reeled through her. She clutched the doorframe as something slithered over her ankles.

She jumped, then realized it had been Wilcox. Keep calm. You're being silly. Following the shadow's direction, Jane moved from window to window and peered at the snow. In the dim light, footprints appeared below the dining room sill. Large prints: a man's. She crept along the wall and through the archway to the foyer.

Before returning to the living room, she flipped off the light. The telephone rang. Quaking, terror clutched her as she gaped at the telephone in the light of the television. Two rings. Three rings. She grasped the receiver.

"Hello." Her voice was a whisper.

"What's wrong, Jane?"

Her hand gripped the receiver. "Someone's hanging around outside, Kyle. And I've been getting calls, but no one talks. I'm scared to death." An intake of breath came through the line.

"Don't panic, Jane. The telephone company's reported tons of line problems tonight with the heavy snow. Maybe it's a lineman checking your pole out back.''

"Maybe, but footprints are under the dining room window."

A lengthy pause hung on the line. "The lineman might be checking the connection to the house. Hang on, and I'll get a car over there to check for a prowler."

She breathed deeply, comforted that Kyle was taking action. "I wish you were—"

"As soon as I'm done, I'll be there," he said as if anticipating her sentence. "We're really busy tonight."

Disappointment mingled with fear. She couldn't expect him to walk off his job for her foolish panic.

"I've been trying to check the files, and Dad promised to see if he can recall anything else. Howard Hirschmann was the informer. That's all Dad could add."

"Hirschmann? That sounds familiar." She pushed her thoughts back in time. "I'll be okay, Kyle. I'm jumpy, that's all."

"Anything happening right now?"

"No calls for a while, except yours. And it's been quiet outside for a few minutes."

"Keep the doors locked, and don't open them for anyone. I'll check with you later. I love you."

"Thanks. And I love you."

"And, Jane…say your prayers."

When she hung up, Kyle's words struck her. Once again, she tried to bear the burden on her own. In the flickering TV light, Jane bowed her head. God had been more than good to her. He'd given her Kyle and his loving family. Certainly the Lord would grant her safety.

Kyle's willingness to leave his career settled in her

mind. Though her mind wanted it to happen, her heart said "no." How could she love Kyle and ask him to give up his profession? She couldn't. She had to have faith.

She saw again the stained-glass windows of Redmond Community Church and the outstretched hands of Christ, saying, "Come unto me ye who are weary and heavy laden." If anyone could protect Kyle…and her, it was God's loving hands.

The telephone's ring ripped through the air. Jane's body reeled with the sound. She closed her eyes, lifted the receiver and managed a "hello."

"Jane, this is Len."

Like a gift, relief rolled through her.

"Celia suggested we pick you up and bring you over here to spend the evening."

Jane smiled. Celia did seem to have a sixth sense. "I've been jumpy, Len. Telephone problems, I think. But the weather's too bad to come out. I'll be fine."

"Just a minute, Jane."

She heard a rustling sound and muffled voices. "Sorry. Celia's bellowing from the bedroom. She won't take no for an answer. Get ready and we'll be there shortly. It'll be more fun than sitting alone."

Though she hated to ask them to go out in the winter storm, Jane longed for company. "Are you sure?"

He chuckled. "Positive. You know Celia. She won't have it any other way."

"Okay, I'll be ready."

When she hung up, relief settled over her. She grabbed the telephone to let Kyle know where she'd be and then gathered her coat and handbag and waited until Len's car lights reflected through the window. Though the old adage "two's company, three's a crowd'' marched through her thoughts, tonight ''three'' sounded wonderful.

Kyle relaxed after Jane called. He'd been out in the snowstorm most of the afternoon, and as he wrote up his reports, he knew now she'd be entertained until he could pick her up later on the way home.

He checked the time, deciding she'd be at Celia's by now and dialed her cell phone, but it rang with no answer. Kyle frowned. Why had she turned it off?

Instead, he opened his wallet and pulled out Celia's telephone number. She answered in two rings.

''Celia, this is Kyle. Can I talk to Jane?''

Dead silence weighted the phone line.

''Celia?'' Kyle's heart skipped a beat.

''Jane's not here, Kyle.'' Celia sounded confused. ''I haven't seen her since school today.''

Fear gripped him. Then what about the call…? ''Jane called and said you and Len were picking her up.''

''Len? No. He and I had a terrible argument last night. I haven't spoken to him.''

Kyle's mind pulled and grasped at fragments of thought. ''Are you sure? Jane said he'd called for you—''

''I haven't talked to him today. Why would he call her and say such a…?'' Panic rose in Celia's voice. ''Kyle, do you—?''

''Yes, that's all I can think. I'll talk to you later, Celia.''

Kyle slammed the telephone on the receiver and dialed his father. The horrible reality fell into place. *Howard Hirschmann. Len Hirsch.*

Chapter Twenty

Using the car's headlights to see, Jane locked the house. Descending the porch stairs, she clung to the railing, but when she hit the sidewalk, her foot slipped from beneath her. She caught herself. As she skidded, her vision was drawn to the large footprints pressed into the snow beneath the front window—a waffle footprint with a round emblem on the heel. A chill ran through her. Kyle's theory was wrong.

The car lights blinded her, and she hurried around and reached for the back door handle. As she did, she heard Len's muffled voice over the engine. "In front, Jane."

She took a step sideways and opened the front door. She eyed the empty seat.

"Climb in," he said, patting the spot beside him.

"Where's Celia?"

He chuckled. "You know her. She wasn't ready, so I said I'd come by myself."

"That's nice of you, Len. Thanks." Jane closed the door, grateful for Celia's friendship.

"Celia said she'd start dinner." He shifted into reverse and backed slowly from the driveway.

"Driving's terrible," Jane commented, grasping for conversation.

"When you're determined, you can do anything."

His tone rang strangely in her ears, but she chided her skittish thoughts. "You're right about that," she said.

The car slipped as he turned the corner, and he adjusted his grip. Though salt trucks rumbled past, the highway appeared glazed and slick. Jane rubbed her neck, feeling edgy and anxiously watched for the familiar landmarks.

When the car passed the expected turn, Jane sidled a look at Len. "Didn't you miss the turnoff?"

He stared straight ahead. "For Celia's, yes, but I have some unfinished business first." He glanced at her. "You don't mind, do you?"

She did, but what difference did it make? She shook her head and stared off into the snowy darkness. They took the ramp onto the interstate, and a panicky feeling swept over her. She didn't want to be out in this storm with Len, running strange errands. Why hadn't he dropped her off at Celia's? They'd been so close.

Her hands lay knotted in her lap, and her icy fingers trembled inside her leather gloves.

"Nervous?" he asked. "You look scared to death."

A laugh raked from his throat that smacked Jane in the pit of her stomach. When she lifted her eyes to his, he squinted at her, an odd glint in his eyes.

"I'm not crazy about this storm. I suppose I'd rather you'd drop me at Celia's."

"I suppose." He chuckled. "But I couldn't do that."

His words nailed her to the seat. Why couldn't he

drop her off first? She feared to ask. In the depth of her mind, images rose. Len had been at the cider mill and the Christmas party. He'd offered to bring her a drink. Later she'd been ill. Instinctively she looked down in the glow of the instrument panel and noticed his heavy boots. Did they have a waffle-pattern sole?

Her heart pounded and her pulse jackhammered in her temple. She struggled to think clearly. The key. Had he had the opportunity to get her house key? Maybe from the rock outside. But did he know about that? Or the day she misplaced her keys at school. They'd hung in her unlocked car all day.

The pumpkin farm? Hiding beneath a scarecrow costume was easy. Her mind flew, thinking of all the encompassing incidents. The razor blade. Celia's key would let him into her classroom. Was she right? And did Celia know about it after all?

She glanced nervously toward him. "Where are we going, Len?"

Clutching her purse in her lap, she heard the chime of her cell phone. She gasped. Kyle. Could she—

"Turn that thing off," Len said, his volume rising.

"But—"

"Off!"

She fumbled in her bag and jammed the power button. The ringing stopped.

"Thank you," he said, his voice like syrup. "We have a little business to take care of, Jane, you little redheaded beauty."

Jane hesitated. Had she misunderstood his intentions? "You shouldn't say that, Len. What about Celia?"

A sick laugh burst from him. "Celia? But, Jane, I only hung out with Celia to learn more about you."

Her memory flew back to Celia and Len's meeting. Had he manipulated their chance meeting at the restaurant? "What are you talking about?"

"I'm talking about you, Jane...and that fiery hair. Just like Red Conroy."

She gasped.

He leered at her.

"What does my dad have to do with anything?"

"He double-crossed my father, Jane. Don't you remember?"

"Your father?" Her mind flew, trying to imagine what he meant.

"Howard Hirschmann. Does the name ring a bell?"

Hirsch. Hirschmann. And *Howard,* the name in the Dick and Jane primer.

"Your father set mine up to be murdered, to cover his own crime. Crooked cops...get away with murder. I've suffered for years. My father took the fall for yours. Red promised my dad anonymity and protection. Instead he betrayed him. Killed him."

"My father was killed, too, Len. My dad was innocent. The stories connecting him to the rackets weren't true. They were a cover-up to protect your dad, not hurt him."

Like a dying leaf in the winter wind, her body trembled without mercy. How could she convince him? "They were both killed. All these years I believed those stories were true. But I found out different. They're not true."

Len sneered at her. The car skidded on the slick pavement. "Does the weather remind you of anything, Jane?" He veered the wheels back to the road.

She froze, remembering the frightening drive to the

hospital the day Kyle had been shot. "How did you know about that night?"

"Heard of a police scanner? Anybody can buy one."

Bile crept to her throat. She swallowed the burning sensation, praying to God for help. "You have to believe me, Len. I've suffered the same as you."

A sick laugh rent the air. "You've suffered just a little more, Jane. But I'm nearly finished. No more suffering. It'll all be over."

All over. "What do you mean?" Her voice tore from her.

"What do you think I mean? I mean all over, no more suffering. Finished. Done. Dead."

Dead. She forced a scream back inside her.

He pulled an envelope from his pocket and dropped it into her lap. She stared at it, not needing to read its horrifying contents.

"Open it." He glared at her with wild, glazed eyes.

She pulled the paper from its housing, her blurred eyes focusing on the familiar block print.

See Jane die.

Her tremors shook the paper from her hand. She snatched it and shoved it out of sight.

She had to think. Remain calm. *Oh, God, help me.*

"I've lived in terror for months. Isn't that enough? Can't we stop now?" Fear rasped her voice.

"For months I sat in a drug clinic trying to put my life back in order. *Months.* For *years,* I lived without a father because of you—your father."

His words spiraled through her mind.

"Without realizing, my old friend Dale Keys told me where you were. I'll never forget the day he came for a visit and mentioned that the art teacher told him a woman teacher had taken over his class at Jackson

Elementary. A Jane Conroy. 'Conroy?' I asked myself. 'Could that be Jane Conroy, daughter of Red Conroy?' And by jingo, it was. I'd never have known. So I came back to the old hometown to watch you suffer.''

Tremors tore through her. She had to escape. If she opened the car door, she'd be killed, but eventually they had to stop. And when they did, she'd run.

Kyle's powerful image rose in her mind. *Dear God, please, send him to me. Lord, You can move mountains.*

"Have I told you why you must suffer, Jane? 'Because I am a jealous God, punishing the children for the sins of the fathers.' God has given me permission to punish you, to rid the world of your suffering. Then I'll rid the world of mine.''

In his madness, Len would never listen to reason. Jane's heart thundered, her pulse raced, her mind tore. *Heavenly Father, I have no way to protect myself. Lord, keep me safe. Forgive my sins, and I pray, Lord, for Your holy protection. In Jesus' name.*

"Amen'' echoed in her terror-filled mind. She closed her eyes, waiting for God's peace to calm her.

Kyle stood, gripping the telephone receiver, his father on the other end of the line. "Check out Union Lake,'' he said to a fellow officer sitting at a computer. "My dad said they met years ago in some cottage there.'' That has to be it. A perfect location. No one around in the winter, and he'd associate the place with his father's meetings with Jane's dad.

The officer glanced at Kyle. "You don't think he'd take her to his home?''

"No chance. This guy's sick. He's preoccupied with the past. Each attack has gotten worse, and he's about as dangerous as he's going to get. Can you find the place?'' A lake. The impossible spiraled into Kyle's mind. His gut ached with panic.

''I'm getting there.'' A map rose on the screen, pinpointing the address Kyle had gotten from the buried informant files. ''Here it is.''

''Print it off. There's an APB to watch for his vehicle. Send them the address.''

Kyle ripped the paper from the printer, and George dashed alongside him to the squad car.

Kyle's mind wrestled with the pieces of information that he'd gathered since he'd spoken to Celia. An image of the cement block lay as heavily on his thoughts as concrete. In frozen fear, the block jettisoned Len's plan into Kyle's mind. If he used the concrete as an anchor, Jane's body would sink to the lake bottom through a hole in the ice. Her remains wouldn't be found for months, if at all. His prayers soared as George sped away from the station house and headed down Telegraph Road toward Union Lake.

Street signs flew past and Jane realized they were headed north. Len's voice jarred her.

''I want to show you where I spent my happier summer days, Jane. On Union Lake. Dad used it as a safe house for meetings with your father. The weather's not good for swimming, but that won't matter.''

Swimming. The cement block bolted into her thoughts, a ludicrous symbol of the mob's body disposal method. Hysteria knotted inside her. Ignoring his chatter, her mind raced, trying to imagine how she might distract him. Anything.

Earlier, they'd left the main highway. The narrow winding roads slanted and turned following Sylvan

Lake, Orchard Lake, Cass Lake, Green Lake. Union Lake had to be near.

As his car swerved and spun down a narrow strip of road, darkness shrouded everything. Summer cabins closed for the winter. Empty. Silent. She shuddered.

Len pulled behind a cottage and slowed, turning off the lights. Ready to bolt, Jane glanced toward the door handle. Before she moved, metal flashed in Len's hand.

"Don't try it, Jane. I don't want to shoot you." He laughed. "But then, it doesn't really matter one way or the other."

In the midst of her frenzied mind, logic found her. Reason told her a bullet was immediate and deadly. Drowning gave her more time to find an escape.

Len brandished the weapon and pulled out a wide roll of gray duct tape. He handed it to her. "Tape your ankles, Jane. Wrap the tape round and round. But first your mouth. Wrap it all the way around."

Struggling to control her fingers, Jane pulled the tape around her mouth and hair, tensing her jaw and face as rigidly as possible, hoping to leave a gap.

He didn't seem to notice in the dark.

She did the same with her ankles, creating tension and pulling them apart as imperceptible as possible.

But Len grabbed the tape and tightly bound her hands in front of her, then wrapped her arms. When she was bound, he leaped from the car. Slipping in the mounds of snow, he darted to the cottage porch and pulled a snow shovel from beneath the flooring. Frantically he dug at the huge snow pile blocking the door of a small shed at the side of the cottage.

Alone, Jane pulled her legs and arms against the tape, trying to loosen it. She scanned for headlights in the side view mirror. Her prayers soared, but nothing came into view.

She turned again to the shed. Len had removed enough snow to open the door. He vanished momentarily, and she twisted her legs, praying to free them, but the tape clung to her pant legs. She remained bound.

Then a motor kicked in, and her heart thundered as a snowmobile shot from the shed and pulled behind her.

In the side view mirror, headlights glared through the windows and silhouettes sprang from a car. With one wrenching motion, she slammed her body against the door lock, praying to delay Len's forcing her outside.

Shouts echoed through the darkness, and a shot rang through the night.

Fear and hope spiraled through her. She pressed herself deep into the seat cushion as sirens and voices screamed in her ears.

The snowmobile motor revved, and tore away.

Gunfire. Glass shattered in the driver's side window. The explosion thundered in her ears. She slid farther toward the floor, praying for safety. With her heart hammering, she heard the chaos move toward the lake.

Lights flashed through the window—blurring red, blue lights circling through her tears. Her chest ached from her thundering heart. Then she heard her name.

"Jane? Where are you?"

Unable to answer, her tears rolled down beneath the edge of duct tape. "Kyle." Her lips formed his name.

The driver's door flew open.

Cringing, Jane looked into the terror-filled eyes of the man she loved.

Kyle hit the unlock button and circled the car, jerking open the door and pulling her into his arms.

Within moments, she stood free beside him, her sobs raking through her body. Kyle's strong, safe arms held her fast, and she heard his whispers of love and thanks to God.

When she gained control of her trembling body, he guided her to the squad car and tucked a blanket around her. He vanished for a moment, then returned.

"It's over, Jane. They have him, wounded but alive."

"He planned to drown me."

"I know. When I realized it was Len, so many things fell into place." He searched her face. "Did he hurt you?"

"No, I'm okay. I prayed so hard. God heard me."

"He heard lots of us. My folks are waiting for us. They've been on their knees since I called them."

Nestled in Kyle's arms on the Mannings' sofa, Jane's exhaustion weighed heavily. After filling in the pieces and rehashing the story, his parents excused themselves. She and Kyle were alone.

Jane cuddled in his arms. Never again would she leave him. Despite the horror of the past months, God had given her a gift. Kyle. How could she doubt that they were meant to be together? She looked into his love-filled eyes, her heart swelling with contentment.

Kyle marveled at Jane's resilience, and his mind raced through the five months since they'd met. Without question, she was God's gift to him. And now, he had a gift to return to her, then his family.

"I'm accepting Kitzmiller's job offer tomorrow, Jane. I know this is a strange time to tell you, but after all this horror, I think you'll be relieved. You told me to do what I had to do, and I think God wants this.''

''God? Are you sure, Kyle? Look in your heart.''

He squirmed, wanting to say it was God, but in truth, he'd made the decision for them. ''You know me too well, Jane. I thought when it came right down to it that you'd be—''

Jane pressed her finger to his lips, silencing him. ''What would I have done without Redmond's finest? Today and through this whole mess, Kyle, you've stood by me, not only because you love me, but because you believe in keeping people safe from harm. I can't take that away from Redmond. And I can't take that away from you.''

Kyle searched her eyes. ''But—''

''There's no 'but' about it. While you were at the station filing the report, I talked to your folks. I told them you'd planned to leave the force, and we've all agreed it'd be a terrible mistake.''

''You talked to my folks?''

She nodded. ''I fought God far too long. If I'd put my faith and trust in the Lord long ago, I wouldn't have suffered all those years. I'd closed my mind and decided things on my own. 'On my own' doesn't work. We need God and we need the people we love. And I love you, Kyle Manning, with all my being. I'm not letting you go. You're handcuffed to my heart.''

He grinned. ''I'm really your prisoner of love.''

''You are,'' she said.

''Then I assume you'll accept my proposal.''

''Proposal for what?'' Her eyes shone with mischief.

He slid to the floor on one knee. ''Jane Conroy, would you do me the honor of marrying me?''

''How could I refuse my knight in blue?'' As he

stood, she clasped his hands and rose beside him. "I accept with all my heart."

Before he could say a word, she silenced him with the most precious kiss he'd ever known.

* * * * *

Be sure to look for
Gail Gaymer Martin's next
Love Inspired novel!
LOVING TREASURES
will be on sale
in June 2002
from Steeple Hill Books.

Dear Reader,

Romance is wonderful. Romance and suspense are supreme. Since childhood, I have been enrapt by mysteries. As an adult, the love has continued, and I find myself drawn to classics like Agatha Christie, Mary Stewart and Ellis Peters's wonderful stories set in an old abbey in twelfth-century England. It was not a surprise, then, when I found myself writing romantic suspense, and Steeple Hill graciously supported me.

As you read Jane and Kyle's story, you watched their struggle to learn about Jane's stalker, and in the process you saw how they learned even more about themselves and their faith.

When troubles come to our doorsteps, I believe that the Lord is helping us grow, to learn and to let go and let God. I pray that in our darkest moments each of us grows in faith, compassion and love just as Jane and Kyle have done in this novel. I hope you enjoyed *A Love for Safekeeping*.

May God bless you.

Gail Gaymer Martin

Next Month From Steeple Hill's™

Love Inspired®

A Perfect Match
by
Deb Kastner

Convinced holy matrimony should be based on more than
romance, Julia Evans believes that she is meant to become the
new pastor's wife. So she is caught off guard when she falls
head over heels for handsome carpenter Zeke Taylor. Can
the man of her dreams also be God's perfect match for her?

Don't miss
A PERFECT MATCH

On sale February 2002

Love Inspired®

Visit us at www.steeplehill.com   LIAPM

Next Month From Steeple Hill's™

Love Inspired®

This Time Forever
by
Carol Steward

The last thing Adam MacIntyre needs is for free-spirited Lisa Berthoff to complicate his life! Although the rugged cowboy is enchanted by the vibrant photojournalist, she doesn't believe in God—or settling down. Can he convince Lisa that she can always come home to his love?

Don't miss
THIS TIME FOREVER

On sale February 2002

Visit us at www.steeplehill.com

LITTF

Next Month From Steeple Hill's™

Love Inspired®

His Healing Touch
by
Loree Lough

During a raging thunderstorm, Kasey Delaney
bounds into Adam Thorne's solitary hideaway.
Bubbling with life, overflowing with enthusiasm for
God's love, the vivacious redhead captivates
Adam's world-weary heart. But the devoted
doctor is hiding behind a shield of guilt that
could shatter Kasey's faith in their love....

Don't miss
HIS HEALING TOUCH

On sale February 2002

Love Inspired®

Visit us at www.steeplehill.com   LIHHT